PUFFIN B

Mac

Neil Arksey lives in London, but spends much of his time in a fantasy world. As well as writing books, he works as an actor. He has a soft spot for his two bikes – a skinny racer and a fat-wheeled off-roader. Other passions include rough-water swimming, surfing (mostly in his dreams), hill-walking, football, sunsets, chess and curling up with a good book.

In memory of
Bobbie C, Matthew H, and Billy McD.
Much loved and now, much missed. Gone the way gooduns always go – too soon, far too soon.

Special thanks to the little gnome *of Highbury.*

Thanks also to:
Katie and the kids and my family,
Barbara Engel from the Royal Hospital's Trust and everybody else who helped.

NEIL ARKSEY

MacB

PUFFIN BOOKS

Another book by Neil Arksey

RESULT!

PUFFIN BOOKS

Published by the Penguin Group
Penguin Books Ltd, 27 Wrights Lane, London W8 5TZ, England
Penguin Putnam Inc., 375 Hudson Street, New York, New York 10014, USA
Penguin Books Australia Ltd, Ringwood, Victoria, Australia
Penguin Books Canada Ltd, 10 Alcorn Avenue, Toronto, Ontario, Canada M4V 3B2
Penguin Books (NZ) Ltd, Private Bag 102902, NSMC, Auckland, New Zealand

On the World Wide Web at: www.penguin.com

Penguin Books Ltd, Registered Offices: Harmondsworth, Middlesex, England

First published 1999
3 5 7 9 10 8 6 4 2

Set in 11½ /14 Palatino

Made and printed in England by Clays Ltd, St Ives plc

British Library Cataloguing in Publication Data
A CIP catalogue record for this book is available from the British Library

ISBN 0-141-30415-4

Fair is foul, and foul is fair . . .

1

FAIR

The ball soared. A pack of boys gave chase, pushing and shoving across the tired-looking grass; one stumbled open-mouthed and fell.

Banksie watched, Mac beside him. Behind them a fairground generator obliterated sound.

'*Nah* . . .' Mac had to yell to make himself heard. 'I don't recognize any of them. Probably travellers . . . came with the fair. Older, don't you reckon?'

Banksie nodded.

'And big. Bigger than me.' Mac grinned. 'Loads taller than you.'

'There's not *that* much difference between us.' Banksie jabbed his mate in the back. 'Watch it – I'm closing the gap all the time.'

'Yeah, sure you are!' Mac nodded towards the ragtag game on the heath. 'Come on – what d'you say?'

'Pretty rough-looking . . . hard-tackling.'

'But you and I could run rings round 'em, *easy*!'

Banksie glanced back at the fair.

'Come on,' said Mac, 'it's not as if that's going anywhere. It'll be more exciting after dark. Let's see if we can't get a game.'

A tall boy charged towards one of the makeshift goals. He shot. The goalie dived the wrong way; the ball rolled across the grass.

Banksie shook his head. 'That lot are getting hammered.'

'You're not wrong! They need us. Come on!' Giving a sharp, shrill whistle, Mac set off at a jog.

The unfamiliar boys watched their approach, sizing them up. One, stocky and dark haired, came forward to meet them.

Flicking the ball up, Mac tapped it sideways.

Banksie caught it on his chest, let it roll down to his foot, flicked it back.

Mac headed it: one, two, three, then dropped it to his instep, a dead ball. He paused for a moment, the ball frozen to his foot, before flicking it up and heading it back.

Banksie controlled the ball with his thigh; bounced it from one leg to the other.

Every day of the holidays, he and Mac had spent hours working on moves and seeking out games together. It had been great. Mac had started at St Dunstan's just after Easter. The end of another disappointing school football season during which, once again, he had *not* been selected for the team. Mac's newcomer's keenness had been just what Banksie had needed to kick-start his own campaign to prepare for this year's team trials. They had traded tricks and techniques. They had developed set pieces. They had pushed each other. Hard.

Banksie twisted sharply and back-heeled the ball straight to Mac's waiting hands. Precise. Not flash. This was the pay-off: polished skills and the two of them together tight as a drum.

Mac nodded at the stranger. 'Thought maybe you could use a couple of extra players?'

'Yeah?' The dark-haired boy glanced back at his friends. They shrugged. He nodded. 'Yeah, all right then.'

'Cool.' Mac flipped the ball.

The boy caught it. 'We're three–one down. Maybe you can make a difference.' Dropping the ball, he kicked it high and long.

Suddenly, players were charging helter-skelter across the grass.

'Come on,' yelled Mac, 'the ball's in play! Let's show them what we're made of!'

*

The full moon drifted under a blanket of cloud. Banksie carefully rolled up the leg of his jeans. In the darkness, the cries and screams from the fair brought to mind a battlefield – images of gory slaughter. He winced, clenching his lip between his teeth. Just his luck – one sliding tackle all afternoon and he had to land on something sharp. He shivered as he touched the cut, tutting himself for his squeamishness. It was sticky now; the blood had congealed nicely. 'Come *on*, Mac!' he hissed. 'I'm getting cold!'

'Sorry!' Mac emerged from behind a tree, struggling with his fly. 'Too much to drink!'

'I'm heading back.' Banksie set off, limping stiffly towards the fair.

Pulsating with music and laughter, the fair was surrounded by an amber fug, an aura of warmth and diesel smell, like a protective force field. Silhouetted against the blur of coloured lights, people came and went between the trucks and caravans. Banksie found himself hurrying.

'On the wing!' Mac's dark shape pounded through the shadows. The reflective strip on his trainers flickered as he shot past. His foot swung. A crumpled can rose, glinted, and dropped into the blackness of the heath.

'Oi!'

'What *idiot* . . .?'

'*Whoops!*' Mac ducked and span away from the voices. They were girls' voices. Angry voices.

'What are you playing at?'

'You could have *maimed* somebody, stupid.'

It was too dark to make out more than shapes.

'Time to scarper,' hissed Mac.

Shrugging apologetically to the night, Banksie turned and hobbled after his friend.

The fair was packed – families, couples, gangs and groups all crowded together, wide eyed, chattering and laughing. Down the avenue of sideshows the movement slowed to a shuffle, one continuous herd, lit by flashing coloured lights. Lifted faces stared, fingers pointed at the squealing riders on the Big Wheel. Loitering around the perimeters of the Waltzers, the Death Ride and the Skydiver, the crowds nudged each other, daring each other to have a go.

With an eye on Mac's bobbing ginger curls, Banksie ducked and squeezed his way through the slow sea of bodies.

'Oi! Watch out, son!'

'Mind whose feet you stand on, why don't you!'

Finally, where a space opened up around a row of hot-dog stalls, Mac slowed.

'Hey – thanks for waiting, partner.' Banksie limped to a halt. 'Not one of your better shots, that last one.'

'Oh, I don't know . . .' Mac smirked. 'I didn't hit anyone!' He gestured towards a row of stalls. 'What do you want to have a go at next? Coconut shy? Shove ha'penny?'

'*Please* – anything but another rifle range.'

'Can't take being beaten?'

'I was unlucky.'

'No, my friend.' Mac slapped him on the shoulder. 'No. *I* am on a roll.' He punched the air triumphantly. 'Three times on the rifles and three beauties in the game against the fairground boys!'

'I might have bagged a hat-trick too,' said Banksie, 'if that vicious git hadn't fouled me.' He glanced down at where blood had darkened his jeans. 'Anyway, I thought we work together?'

'Yeah – we do,' Mac grinned, 'on the field. But I still beat you on the rifles!'

'You were lucky.' Banksie bit his lip. He didn't like it when Mac came on so full of himself. They were supposed to be partners, at least that had been the plan – their hard training together was going to give them the edge over the others in the school trials. But Mac had to be best at everything.

'Luck wasn't in it!' chuckled Mac. 'I beat you

again.' His green eyes glinted with excitement. 'Then I lost one of my pellets – that was *unlucky* – but still I beat you a third time!'

'Yeah, OK,' Banksie threw up his hands. 'I get the message. But there was nothing hardly between us.'

Mac laughed and draped an arm across his friend's shoulders. 'According to you, there never is. A beating's a beating, mate! Admit it: I am the best shot.'

'The sights on my rifle were way off.'

'And mine *weren't*?'

'It took me a while to get used to them.'

'Ah!' Mac chuckled. 'But finally you did. And then you still lost. Very good!' He aimed an imaginary rifle. 'With my deadly aim, I could earn a fortune as an assassin.'

'Yeah, right.' Banksie sneered. 'If you weren't already tipped as the nation's number-one striker.'

'You said it!' Nothing was going to shift Mac's self-confident good humour. He laughed. 'Maybe I could do the assassinations in my spare time!'

'Of course . . . travelling abroad with the national squad, you'll just slip away, quietly bump off some evil terrorist or whatever, then rejoin the lads for a training session, with nobody any the wiser.'

'You missed out the bit about scoring the winning goal!' Mac clasped his hands above his head.

'Oh yeah.' Banksie sighed and shook his head. 'My good mate, destined for greatness.'

'Oi, Goldilocks!'

The two boys spun round.

2

FATE

'Oi, Goldilocks!'

Shanice. Banksie watched his sister approach, flanked by two girlfriends.

'That was *us* your stupid friend nearly hit with a can.'

Dark-eyed Nina shook her raven curls. Cropped tomboy, Eve, chewed gum.

'It just missed Nina's head.'

Mac was smirking.

'Your friend is a *turnip*.'

'Total.' Banksie tapped his skull. 'He can't help it.'

'You might at least teach the idiot some manners,' said Shanice, 'if you're going to hang around with him.' She glowered at Mac. 'Too cool to say sorry, I suppose?'

Mac shrugged.

Shanice shook her head and turned to her brother. 'So, sampled anything exciting?'

'The rifle range . . .'

'Intrepid!' Shanice laughed. 'Is that *it*?'

Banksie felt himself blush. 'Yeah, so far – apart from toffee apples and hot dogs.'

'The rifle range!' Shanice turned to her girlfriends. 'What is it about boys and guns? Adventurous, or what!'

Eve and Nina shook their heads.

'The Big Wheel.' Shanice pointed. 'The Wall of Death, the Skydiver – haven't you been on *any* rides?'

Mac snorted. 'Kids' stuff.'

'Oh really, danger-boy?' Shanice turned. 'Too tame for you? Not up to the thrills of blindly kicking cans in the dark?'

Mac shrugged.

'He's so tough!' purred Nina

Eve growled. 'I bet he had *mustard* on his hot-dog!'

'Are you kidding?' Shanice made wide eyes. 'This guy has chilli on his breakfast!'

The girls laughed.

Stifling a grin, Banksie glanced at his mate. Shanice and her friends could rip the best to shreds. If only Mac would keep his mouth shut.

'Put it this way –' Mac jabbed the air with his finger – 'nothing at this fair could scare me.'

Shanice glanced at her girlfriends. 'Is that a fact?'

Mac puffed out his chest. 'Uh-huh.'

Shanice studied him. 'Ever been to a fortune teller?'

Mac snorted. 'You're joking, aren't you? Gypsy Rosa Lee?'

'No, actually,' said Shanice, 'I'm not joking. And no, it isn't Gypsy Rosa *anything*.' Her eyes pierced. 'Oh, but fortune telling's kids' stuff too, I suppose?' She aimed an imaginary gun at Mac's chest. 'Mr Reckless Cool . . . ' Slowly, she tightened her finger on the invisible trigger. 'Mr Sharp Shooter . . .'

PooOOSssssh!

'He flinched!' shrieked Nina.

'It was a *twitch*,' snapped Mac.

'You practically *jumped*.' Shanice laughed, pointing. 'At some hydraulic, hissing thing on that ride!'

The girls' shrill laughter rose above the noise of the fair.

Mac folded his arms across his chest.

Shanice walked over. 'What are you afraid of, danger-boy?' She spoke quietly, just inches from his face.

'Nothing.'

They stared.

'Really!' Shanice shook her head, smiled and leant closer. 'Then go visit the fortune teller. Go on, if you're so fearless. I *dare* you. Here –' She placed a five-pound note on his folded arms – 'you and my brother. My treat!'

Mac screwed up the note and flung it back.

Letters painted large on the side of the caravan spelt: DESTINY.

At the top of the steps, Mac paused and peered inside. 'This is *your* doing.'

Banksie shook his head. 'Dug your own grave, mate.'

'You agreed with your sister!'

'It was hard not to, the way you were carrying on. Anyway she owed me a fiver.'

Mac scowled and stepped inside.

Banksie followed. The room was small. There were chairs, the lighting was dim.

Mac sniffed. '*Ugh!*' He pulled a face.

'Incense,' explained Banksie. He recognized the smell from his sister's bedroom.

'I was expecting you . . .'

Both boys jumped. The voice, a woman's, came from behind a bead curtain.

'Please . . . come through, boys.'

Banksie returned Mac's stare. Pulling aside the beaded strands, he bowed to his friend. 'After you.'

They entered.

The small, dark room was strangely, eerily

hushed, as if the fairground noises had been somehow absorbed by the gloom.

'Soundproofing.' A candle flickered. The owner of the warm, husky voice stepped out from behind a partition. The candle moved with her, lighting her face – strong cheekbones, full lips, glistening braids. She smiled, lowering the candle in a gesture towards the table. 'Please – come and sit. Make yourselves at home.'

'How did you . . .?' Mac sounded edgy.

The woman laughed, gently. 'Read your mind?'

Mac nodded.

'It was an easy guess. The fairground's noisy – silence is the first thing strangers notice when they enter. I need peace for my work.' Reaching up, she adjusted the light above the table. It hissed; its soft greenish glow grew brighter, pushing back the shadows. 'Gas*sss*light . . .' The hiss of her voice mingled with the hiss of the gas. 'Limelight – so much prettier and friendlier than electric, don't you think? Please – sit.'

Banksie gave his friend a nudge. He pulled back a chair. 'You knew we were coming,' he said.

The woman's smile broadened, showing large white teeth. 'Let's say, I had an inkling.'

The teeth were like tombstones. Banksie

stared – the woman's widening eyes began to *glow* a strange green colour. He gulped.

'Don't be alarmed,' the woman chuckled, 'my contact lenses catch the light.'

Banksie felt his stomach tighten.

Mac shifted in his seat. 'So –' he cleared his throat – 'no crystal ball?'

The woman shook her head. 'I've never shown much affinity.' She cupped an imaginary ball with her hands. 'Basic ball skills can be picked up so easily, don't you think? But real talent's a different matter – either you've got it, or you haven't.'

Banksie felt the eyes flicker – from Mac to him, and back again. An eyebrow arched.

'Wouldn't you agree?'

Mac opened his mouth, but there was no sound. He nodded.

She chuckled softly. 'Oh, I have *talent*, but not the sort that works through crystal. Eyes and hands are my tools.' She rubbed her palms together in a slow, circular action, smooth and rhythmical. 'Magic is all around us, it suffuses the globe. I've borrowed here and there, from everywhere: Voodoo, Obeah, African, Romany, Druid. I stick to the bedrock stuff: dice, runes, tarot, lifelines.'

The movement of the woman's hands was hypnotic. She turned her palms upwards and spread her forearms on the table. Her skin glowed warm mahogany against the darker wood.

'A seer must be versatile. She needs to be fluid. She's a medium. Spirits speak *through* her and *to* her.' The fingers beckoned. 'Give your hands to Hecate.'

Mac frowned.

'My spirit name,' said the woman, stretching her hands closer. 'Come.'

Banksie and Mac each took hold of a hand.

'Each other's too,' she said. 'Now – of what do you wish to learn: past, present or future?'

Mac and Banksie glanced at one another.

'All three?' said Banksie.

'You may choose only one.'

'Then it's got to be the future,' said Mac. 'We know about the past and the present.'

The woman nodded. Slowly, she bowed her head. 'If, whilst I'm talking, I describe anything either of you recognize as having relevance, squeeze my hand to let me know.'

Banksie felt a faint tingling sensation where her palm touched his. A moment later . . . the same feeling only fainter in his other palm. Mac was staring wide-eyed – he had felt it too.

'I sense . . .' said the woman, '. . . I sense a tight-knit group of boys . . . they're wearing uniforms . . . no, rather they are uniformly dressed . . . a gang . . . or perhaps more organized than that – a *team*? Yes, some kind of team.'

Banksie squeezed.

'Aah!' The woman raised her head and gave a low chuckle. 'Both of you recognize this image. That's good. I'm on the right track.' She inclined her head once more. 'I'll try to go deeper. Please shut your eyes. Focus your mind. Let us see what we can find.'

As Banksie closed his eyes, the gas lamp's hiss seemed to grow louder. He fought the urge to fidget. His arms felt heavy, he wanted to stretch and flex them. The woman's hand felt hot; Mac's felt like ice. Taking a long slow breath, he tried to obey the request to 'focus'. The school team – was Mac concentrating on it too? He had to be. Getting in that team meant *everything*.

'The team,' said the woman, 'is a football team.'

Banksie squeezed her hand again.

'There are lots of boys . . . all eager to join, it's very important to them. It's very important to you. Competition is fierce.'

'Do we get in?' blurted Mac.

'I see you playing . . .' said the woman.

'We play all the time,' said Banksie. 'What are we wearing?'

'What colour shirts?' said Mac.

'Let me see . . .' said the woman. 'How strange . . . the shirts don't seem to have colour.'

'No colour?' said Banksie. 'But we *are* wearing shirts? Could it be they're white?'

The woman made a tutting noise. 'Of course! How foolish of me! That's why – the sun is shining and the shirts you're both wearing are dazzling white.'

'St Dunstan's!' said Mac.

Banksie felt Mac pinch his hand. He sneaked a glance. Mac winked then shut his eyes again.

'The team's captain,' muttered the woman, 'has to be replaced.'

'Replaced . . .' echoed Mac, '. . . who by?' He leant forward, barely able to contain his excitement. 'Who comes after him? Can you see? Is it one of *us*?'

The woman frowned. 'Both of you.'

'Both?'

'Going deeper now . . .' said the woman, 'further into your future, deeper into your destiny . . .' Her frown sharpened; darkened.

Banksie closed his eyes.

'The field won't always be so sunny . . .' A graver tone had crept into her voice. 'I see shadows lurking. I see storm clouds gathering. There is mud now . . . and *blood* on those pure-white shirts.'

Banksie felt himself tense.

'Blood . . .' The woman groaned. *'. . . and mud. Mud and blood!'* Her voice had become a low, rumbling rasp. *'Beneath this table,'* she muttered, *'below our feet, lies a point where two paths meet.'* The rhythm of her words grew stronger, like a chant. *'Where ley lines cross, they double force. Now let this power reveal your course.'*

The gas lamp's background hiss seemed to swell. Banksie's heart was racing. He glanced at Mac. Wasn't there a new sound, a whisper in that hiss? Mac's eyes were open again too, he was listening for something.

'Mud and blood . . . blood and mud!'

Banksie peered. Was that the woman's voice? Her lips weren't moving.

'Against all odds, two friends hold sway
Giants on the field till the darkest day.
One captains first, the other thereafter
One burns fiercest, the other – brighter.'

A sharp gust of wind buffeted the caravan. The gas lamp extinguished with a pop.

'Blood and mud . . .' gasped the voice in the darkness, *'. . . mud and blood!'*

3

TRIALS

'Penalty!'

The whistle blew.

'No way was it!'

Marshall, playing for the reserves, had brought down Dunk from behind, just outside the box.

On rickety benches, laid end to end along the pavilion veranda, upwards of thirty boys sat watching. Nerves had stifled conversation to grunts, growls and the occasional comment.

Banksie piggled the scab on his knee. He and Mac hadn't talked about the fortune teller. Had they both been too shaken? Neither would dare admit it. Or was it because some of what she'd told them had sounded spookily believable, but too good to hope for? Or because much of it had been peculiar, ridiculous or totally impossible? They both thought it was rubbish, didn't they? Didn't they? It had been several days now. The silence felt uncomfortable.

According to the pavilion clock the game had been underway for fifty-three minutes. Banksie sighed. At this rate, he and Mac were going to spend the whole afternoon on the bench. So much for prophesies of glory.

Mr Powell, form English teacher and football coach to the Year, pointed at the spot for the kick. Just outside the box. Perfect for a well-judged curler. Yelling and waving, the reserve team and their goalie argued about the defensive line.

Mac snorted. 'Who are they trying to kid!'

A chorus of grunts expressed agreement.

'The firsts have only scored five,' muttered a voice. 'We *might* keep it out.'

Mac spat on the ground. 'I'm talking about Dunk and his poodles, stupid.' He pointed.

Duncan King, the golden boy: top goal scorer and team captain two years running – tall, fair and exuding the confidence of an all-round athlete. Donatello Cappri with jutting jaw and stocky shoulders. And long-limbed Melvin Thomas, polished skull gleaming like a new conker. The first team's three forwards huddled around the ball, discussing strategies for the kick.

Mac chuckled. 'Who are *they* trying to kid!'

'Yeah!' concurred a voice from the far end of the veranda. 'As if Dunk's going to let someone else take it!'

'As if.'

'With *his* track record.'

'He gets enough opportunities,' muttered Mac.

Another chorus of grunts.

Banksie sighed. 'At this rate, some of us are never going to get a look-in.' He glanced along the bench at the restless fidgets and nail biters. There was a doggy expectant look about each – taut bundles of nerves, *aching* for a chance to perform, to prove themselves. You could almost see the tails wagging: pick me next, their faces said, pick me, pick *me*! Waiting for the nod.

Mr Powell had promised them all an opportunity. Last year's first team were playing against a 'reserve' side selected from the large pool of boys still dreaming of first-team glory. At intervals, Mr Powell substituted from the bench. A player brought on in defence one minute, might find himself up front the next. Playing against the year's elite, this makeshift team of hopefuls had so far, not surprisingly, demonstrated all the skill and tactical awareness of a cluck of headless chickens. More than half those on the bench still hadn't been called on to play.

With the reserves' defensive line finally arranged, Mr Powell blew the whistle. The bench held their breath as Dunk took his run at the ball. Arcing round the last man on the line, it slipped past the keeper's dive and into the back of the net.

'Whoa!'

'Unbelievable!'

'What a bender!' Banksie was on his feet with the others. 'Practically a right angle!'

Mr Powell had blown the whistle. As Dunk made his way towards the pavilion, Don and Mel hung close. The other players, first-teamers in their all-white strip, reserves in grey shirts and red bibs, jostled to pat him on the back or offer praise.

'*Poodles.*' Mac practically spat the word. He panted and sniffed low like a dog.

'They're not stupid.' Banksie watched Mel and Don laughing at Dunk's jokes. 'We'd do the same.'

'We shouldn't need to,' hissed Mac. 'We're better than those two.'

Banksie shrugged.

Studded boots clattered on the pavilion steps. The flushed players crowded up on to the veranda, vying for space on the benches, crouching or flopping on the hard floor.

'Excellent work, King.' Mr Powell nodded to

Dunk. 'The team are having a good game. Let's keep it up in the second half.' He studied his clipboard. 'OK. Time for some new opposition. Stick your hand up – who haven't I seen?'

'Sir!'

'Sir!'

Arms shot up. Mr Powell's eyes flickered along the row. 'Ah! Some familiar faces.' Back to the clipboard. 'Yes. Banks and MacBride. Two of the back-row boys from my English class. Sitting together again, I see. Inseparable, perhaps? Do we play together on the pitch?'

'Yes, sir.' Mac jumped up. 'We've played together loads, sir. Up front.'

'We know each other blind,' said Banksie.

'Uh-huh.' Mr Powell nodded. 'Right- or left-footed?'

'Mac's right, I'm left, sir.'

'OK, I'd like you playing left back.' Mr Powell made a note on the clipboard. 'MacBride, you play over at right.'

'Right *back*, sir? But, sir! Banksie and me – we're forwards, sir. We play as paired strikers.'

'Everyone wants to be a star, MacBride. Unfortunately not all of us have the talent. Duncan King has come up with the goods two years running. And as long as he's able to score goals of this afternoon's calibre, he'll continue to play striker and be captain.' Mr Powell pointed to the bench. 'If I let this lot have their way, they'd all be playing up front. These trials are for me to make my assessment of your abilities. It would help me if you could just play where I ask.'

Mac bowed his head.

'Thank you,' said Mr Powell. 'Now, who else have I still to see?'

At first it was a frantic, haphazard struggle for the two new backs. But, little by little, their shared intuition, ball confidence and awareness of attack strategy made up for a lack of defensive experience.

Banksie whistled. Mac had the ball. Absolute determination that Don and Mel should not get passes through to Dunk was driving Mac and him to better and better play. Mr Powell had been forced to take notice.

Don lunged angrily – this was not the first time Mac had taken the ball off him. Mel charged across to assist. But Mac stayed cool, dancing his feet over the ball, tempting the two agitated players to come forward – teasing them, toying with their frustration.

Banksie slipped into open space behind Don and Mel.

'Come and get it!' Mac goaded.

Don and Mel lunged. Mac pushed the ball

between them. 'Go, Banksie!' he yelled. 'Go on, *go for it*, mate!'

Banksie took off running, looking for gaps and someone unmarked. Where were they? Mac was behind him, following fast. First-team players were homing in. There was nothing else for it. 'Back me up!' he yelled, putting on pace.

Snaking left, then right, he bypassed two. Out on the wing, Marshall's arm shot up as he pulled away from his all-white marker. Banksie lofted the ball and pushed forward. To his right, Mac steamed towards the goal. Mr Powell, whistle in hand, was not far behind. The first team were on the hop! *If he'd just let them keep going . . .*

Up in the left corner, ten yards from the goal line, Marshall hit trouble. Collins, playing striker for the reserves, was making a hash of giving support. Penned in by three of the first team, Marshall did his best to hang on to the ball.

Banksie sprinted to the touchline. 'Pass it back!'

Twisting and turning, Marshall found an opening between the legs. He poked the ball through. But a harsh kick brought him down.

'Foul!'

'Was never!'

Banksie collected. Mr Powell was signalling

play on. The green light! Goal in his sights, he charged.

Suddenly, there were white shirts everywhere, running helter-skelter – backwards, forwards, sideways. The first-team defenders had enjoyed an easy game of it till now. Now it was time for *revenge*.

The tackles came thick and fast. Banksie jumped, dodged, skipped and swerved. As he zigzagged across the pitch, he took a bearing on the one red bib in the box.

'Man on!'

Banksie sensed a body come up beside him, matching his stride.

'Nice . . . run.' Dunk's panting voice.

Banksie pumped his arms and legs harder. An arm and shoulder juddered and churned against his own. He pushed back.

Dunk grunted and *shoved*.

Banksie crashed back hard, flicking the ball just a moment before Dunk's ankle brought him down. The two of them tumbled. Banksie rolled, bounced and staggered to his feet, keeping forward momentum. He looked around.

Mac had the ball.

Mac was charging towards the goal.

'Yes!' Mac had scored!

4
HEATH

Rides had been packed away, caravans and generator trailers hitched to the back of huge trucks. Engines had chugged into life and the long slow convoy had finally lumbered off the heath. A few stragglers remained, but the fair had gone on its way.

The sun cast its low light through the trees. Banksie and Mac mooched, kicking their way through the left-behind litter.

'You played well,' said Banksie.

'Thanks.' Mac smiled and gave him the thumbs up. But his voice was flat. 'You didn't do too badly yourself.'

'Moi?'

'Yeah. You played excellently. We both did.'

Banksie grinned.

'But don't go getting your hopes up.' Mac hacked at the ground with his heel. 'We both know how it works.'

'Yeah . . .' Banksie kicked at a half-eaten toffee apple.

'Mr Powell's not about to tinker with a winning format.' Mac booted the toffee apple hard. It disintegrated.

'Dunk's bound to have a say.'

'And we'll be lucky if we get to sit on the subs bench.'

The two friends continued their trawl through the litter in silence. So far, their search for coins had come up with nothing. They were close to the spot where the fortune teller's caravan had stood. Banksie slowed to a shuffle. 'All that stuff,' he said, 'about this being a special site where ley lines cross and all that . . .'

'Mumbo-jumbo,' said Mac, 'all of it. Fortune tellers are just con artists.'

'Yeah, I reckon,' said Banksie. He felt lighter: happy to have at last broken the ice, relieved by Mac's cynicism. 'You have to admit, though, she picked up on the football connection straight away.'

'Pretty safe guess – boys our age.' Mac kicked a bottle. 'There were probably tell-tale signs: grass and blood stains on our jeans, that sort of thing.'

'What about her hint you might be picked for a team?'

'And *you,* remember!' Mac laughed. 'She was just telling us what she knew we wanted to hear. White shirts? Fat chance! She must have got her ley lines twisted!' Suddenly, his expression changed.

'What?' Banksie jerked round.

Three familiar female figures emerged from the trees.

'Well!' Shanice grinned. 'If it isn't the future heroes of St Dunstan's!'

'The fantastic forwards!' sneered Eve.

Nina chuckled. 'Duncan King's right- and left-hand men.'

Mac glowered.

Banksie sighed and forced himself to take a deep breath.

Arms folded, shoulder to shoulder, the three girls blocked their path.

Mac frowned. 'Where did you appear from?'

Shanice nodded towards the copse. 'Nina spotted you.'

'We were down on Heath Street,' said Eve.

'But that's right over the other side.' Mac looked suspiciously from face to face.

'All that glorious red hair,' chuckled Nina, 'aflame in the dying light.'

Mac blushed.

'We shouted several times,' said Shanice.

'But, whatever you were doing, you were far too engrossed.'

'So you chased all this way after us,' said Banksie, 'just to wind us up?'

'We *never* chase after boys,' said Nina, 'especially ones your age.'

'And we're not winding you up,' said Shanice.

'You were dawdling,' said Eve. 'We took the short cut through the wood.'

'You don't seem very pleased by our news,' said Shanice. She pouted and brushed Mac's lapel with her fingertips.

Mac stiffened.

'You never told me,' she sighed, 'how was your date with Destiny?'

A grin cracked Mac's stony face. 'The fortune teller's? Banksie and me was just saying what a waste of time it was. Phoney, garbled, gobbledygook.'

'About?' said Shanice.

Mac shrugged. 'Just nonsense. A waste of money.' He grinned. 'Though not mine – thankfully!'

'She didn't tell you anything interesting about yourselves?' Shanice widened her eyes. 'No profound, life-changing revelations?'

Mac shook his head.

'That's a shame,' said Eve.

'Never mind.' Shanice shrugged and smiled. 'The two of you have been selected for the soccer team.'

'To play up front with Duncan King,' sighed Nina. 'That should make you happy.'

'Yeah, right!' said Mac.

'Nice try, girls,' said Banksie.

'You don't believe us?' Shanice scowled. 'Then go and ask Duncan yourself. He and some other boys were having an argument about the team selection, down on Heath Street. That's how we found out.'

'You must think we're really stupid,' said Mac.

Shanice shrugged and smiled. 'That's beside the point.'

'Come on!' Banksie grabbed Mac's sleeve. 'I know where Dunk lives. We can cut across the heath.' He jabbed a finger at Shanice. 'I know you're lying!'

'Right,' said Shanice. 'That'll be why you're going to check, then.'

'Jeez!' Mac whistled through his teeth.

'I know,' said Banksie.

'Dunk lives *here*?'

Banksie nodded. 'Posh or what!'

'Must be worth a fortune!'

At the end of the short, gently twisting drive,

trees and bushes gave way to a large open space. Completely hidden from the road, a rather grand house glowed soft peach in the sunset. Tall shiny-barked trees framed the house in burnished copper. A Mercedes and a Jag gleamed on the gravel forecourt.

In front of the garage, a mountain bike balanced on its back. Kneeling on the gravel, a spanner in each hand, Dunk frowned with concentrated effort.

Banksie coughed.

'Guys!' Dunk stood to greet them. 'What brings you here? You must have heard something, right?'

Mac and Banksie glanced at one another. Mac nodded. 'Banksie's sister –'

'My sister,' Banksie interrupted, 'is the world's greatest wind-up artist.'

Dunk grinned. 'What's she said?'

'The thing is . . .' Banksie chuckled, 'she and her stupid mates claim we've been picked to play alongside you.'

'You don't believe them?' said Dunk. 'After your performances at the trials, Mr Powell asked how I'd feel about sticking you two in the starting line-up for Wednesday's friendly. As a try out.' He shrugged. 'I told him – yeah. He was going to tell you tomorrow. Your sister and her friends must have heard me breaking the news to Mel and Don – there was a bit of a rumpus.'

'Don't suppose they were too happy,' said Mac.

Dunk shrugged. 'Kind of to be expected – they fed me balls all last season. But you guys played excellently, and you worked so well together.' He nodded to Mac. 'You're good. I've only ever seen you play in the yard till now – and it's difficult to get an idea from that. But I remember Banksie from last year's practice games and trials. He's always been a good little worker.'

'Cheers.'

'I mean it – you've improved no end.'

'We're in the same form,' said Banksie.

'Like Don, Mel and me,' said Dunk. 'It's daft the way we all have our separate games in the yard.'

Banksie nodded. 'Mac doesn't live too far from me. We played practically all summer together.'

'Well – it's paid off. If Wednesday goes well, you're likely to get played again. Look at Mr Cartwright last year – played the same players all season through.'

'Yeah.' Banksie grunted. 'Don't remind me.'

'Mr Powell's different,' said Dunk. 'Mr Cartwright was basically lazy – as long as St

Dunstan's kept winning, he didn't have to bother. Luckily for him I kept scoring right through the season. Mr Powell is the sort that wants to try new ideas. That's good – keeps all of us on our toes. There'll be more team changes, I guarantee, before the season's over.'

Mac grinned. 'You better watch out, then!'

Dunk nodded.

The three boys laughed.

A sing-song woman's voice called from the house.

Dunk shrugged. 'Sounds like I'm needed.'

Banksie nodded. 'It's getting dark, we should be chipping.'

They touched fists.

'I'm looking forward,' called Dunk, from the front door.

Under the canopy of trees, the drive was now in darkness. The two boys sprinted to the road.

First by a nod, Mac thundered to a halt at the gate. Banksie stopped beside him, bent over, panting.

'It's happening . . .' gasped Mac, suddenly.

'What?' Banksie looked up. 'What is?'

'The prophesy.'

'Oh, yeah – of course!' Banksie chuckled. *'The prophesy.'*

'I'm serious.' Mac frowned. 'This is the start of what she predicted.'

Banksie stared. In flickering shadow, Mac's face seemed to twist and darken.

Mac chuckled. 'Admit it . . .' He stepped out under the street lamp's amber. 'I had you for a moment there!'

'Yeah – right!' Banksie made a face. 'Like I really *believed* you.'

5
FRIENDLY

'It's not quite the scoreline I would have hoped for at half time, but –' Mr Powell closed the dressing-room door – 'I'm not unduly worried. Two out of their three goals were lucky. We've been the better side. I'm confident we can beat them.'

In the centre of the room, he took up a now familiar stance: straight back, arms folded, feet apart. 'McAllister and MacBride . . .' He eyed each in turn. 'McA and MacB. Why might I single you out for comment? Any ideas?'

Banksie looked over. Mac was scowling at his boots.

Mr Powell paced the dressing-room floor.

'How about you, McA?'

McAllister shrugged. 'I keep forgetting to mark?'

'You keep forgetting to mark.' Mr Powell

nodded. 'At least you know where you're going wrong. And what might you do to rectify the situation in the second half?'

'Mark?'

'Excellent, McA.' Mr Powell turned. 'MacB . . .'

'Sir.'

'What about you, MacB?'

'Sir?'

'Anything you might do in the second half to increase the chances of a St Dunstan's victory?'

Mac's eyes remained firmly fixed on his boots. He shrugged.

Mr Powell stood over him. 'No ideas?'

'More feeding, maybe.'

'More . . .?'

'More *feeding*, sir.'

'Yes, MacB. Good. *More feeding*. You and Banks are fitting in well . . .'

Banksie felt the glances of his teammates.

'The pair of you have been doing a good job.' Mr Powell smiled. 'You've communicated and co-operated splendidly. But you might want to take a leaf from Banks's book – he rarely comes so far forward, yet consistently he delivers more balls to our front man.'

Banksie felt himself blush.

'You are *not* a striker in this team, MacB.' Mr Powell frowned. 'A couple of your feeder balls have looked distinctly like shots on goal.

Instead of taking the ball right up to the front line, instead of dribbling your way in every time, how about some early passes?' He pointed to Dunk. 'King is always there, waiting for those balls. If you deliver them sooner, there's less chance of an interception.'

'I'm not deliberately hanging on to it, sir. It's my style.'

'New teams and new roles take a bit of getting used to,' said Mr Powell. 'I appreciate that. You've shown bags of confidence, a good attacking style and great ball control. But in the second half – more passing, less running with the ball. And let's have those all-important through-balls a touch earlier. Look for the long ones. Above all, we want *more in the box*.'

'For Dunk to bang home.'

'Precisely,' said Mr Powell.

The blue shirts of Russell Park retreated hastily. The tide was turning. The long shot, only their third attempt to press forward this half, had been well wide of the mark.

As Gregg prepared to take St Dunstan's goal-kick, Banksie sidled towards a space on the wing. Scanning the field, Gregg dummied to McAllister on the right. The strong, high kick that followed, wrong-footed players on both sides. The ball soared deep.

Banksie knew it was a good one. Setting off at a side-gallop, he watched the ball descend in a perfectly judged arc. The smallest of touches brought it to his feet, without even a change of pace.

Time now to take advantage! Time to make up the deficit. Well positioned to receive, Mac was signalling for the ball. But before Banksie could make the pass, Russell Park's blue shirts swarmed, like flies round a jam pot.

'Close him down!'

Banksie shimmied and side-stepped a tackle; he twisted to throw off a second; but the blue shirts kept coming. They were hemming him in. With nowhere else to go, he cut sharply towards the centre, searching for flashes of St Dunstan's all-white.

'Played, Banks!' Mr Powell pointed from touchline. 'Find your man.'

In the box, Dunk was trying to shake off a couple of defenders. Behind him, Mac's red hair glowed like a cigarette end. Banksie lofted the ball to his partner, and headed towards the goal.

Crossing the ball straight back, Mac pushed forward to receive in return.

'That's the stuff,' yelled Mr Powell. 'Good man, MacB. And again!'

Mac signalled. Chipping the ball, Banksie

bypassed the defender and ran on, slipping it through the legs of a second, straight to Mac.

One touch, Mac tapped it back again.

Banksie looked up. Dunk was there, straight ahead, perfectly positioned, running in. He fed the ball through.

'Tackle him!' roared the opposition's coach. 'Come on! *Defend!*'

It was all over too quickly. Dunk slipped round one, barged a clumsy second, and fired.

'Yes!' Banksie punched the air.

In off the crossbar. The goalie never had a chance.

'This is more like it, St Dunstan's!' On the touchline, Mr Powell cupped his hands and emptied his lungs. *'Come on, now! Keep up the pressure!* There's still time to win this one.'

Banksie checked his watch as Dunk ran up alongside. 'Three or four minutes,' he panted, 'five at the most.'

Mac spat. 'The way they've been playing, they're going to hang on for the draw.'

'We *have* to get that ball,' said Dunk. *'You* guys have to. I'll be waiting.'

The three boys took up positions. The whistle blew. Just as Mac had predicted, Russell Park moved the ball across the field and back – not even a pretence of attack.

early days – the start of my first full year at the school and I've already managed to get picked for the team. That's not bad for a newcomer.'

'"Not bad for a newcomer" – you see!' Mrs MacBride sneered. Her voice was rising: higher and louder. 'That's just what I'm talking about – making allowances for yourself. Your father was the same: always justifying everything, always coming up with an excuse. He even had one, I don't doubt, to justify walking out on me and my three-month-old baby son.'

Banksie chewed a sliver of fingernail. Mac's ashen face left no doubts: the moment described had been his last time with his father.

'Comparing me like that, isn't fair!' snapped Mac. 'I'm not saying getting in the team is *all* I want. You know it's not. I'm as good as the best of them, better than most. I want to be captain.'

'What happened to "I'm going to be captain"?'

'I am. I am going to be.'

'Not if you don't score goals, you're not. Not if you don't get picked for a proper match.'

'Give me a chance! I told you . . .'

'*No!*' Mrs MacBride's tone silenced her son.

Banksie shivered.

'*I* am telling *you*.' Mrs MacBride's piercing dark eyes had Mac skewered to his seat. She advanced. 'I want to be *proud* of my son. I want

'*Pressurize!*' yelled Mr Powell. 'The game is yours, St Dunstan's. Come on – take it!'

Dunk charged a midfielder with such explosive speed, the boy panicked and hoofed the ball. Russell Park kept possession, St Dunstan's pressed forwards.

The ball was slipped out to the right. Now Mac dashed forwards to harass. He followed the ball, snarling as it was passed back and across.

'Come on, Russell!'

'Come on, St Dunstan's!'

Banksie moved up. The penalty area was becoming crowded.

Dunk harried again. Again the ball was played back. Mac moved in on the right.

'Keep your heads!' yelled Russell Park's stocky captain. 'Man on!'

Mac tackled hard and late, he sprawled with his victim. But the ref signalled *play on* to the blues. Eager to clear the ball, a skinny defender booted it high and wide.

'Mine!' Banksie charged. Two Russell Park players had the same idea. The ball was falling. He leapt – rising to meet it, full velocity, with a sharp down-nod of the head – and landed running, staggering, chasing the ball he had barely controlled.

'Get stuck in!'

'Flatten him!'

Banksie turned sharply towards the centre, twisting and swerving as tackles followed in quick succession – early, late, high – Russell Park desperate and panicking.

Dunk was bobbing and weaving on the edge of the box, giving defenders the runaround. Mac, further back, was putting the jitters up the midfield. Banksie pointed and passed.

'Go *on*, St Dunstan's!'

Mac dodged and barged his way through. With the ball at his feet, he shoved some more, driving forward through an onslaught.

'And again, MacB!' Mr Powell's voice floated across the field. *'Use your teammates.'*

'Banksie!' Mac toe-tapped it back.

Banksie lurched, braked and returned it through the legs.

Mac hurdled a tackle and chipped the ball forward.

Dunk was there, already accelerating. He swerved and blasted . . .

'Ye-e-e-e-e-sss!'

Ecstasy.

A bright-green sports bag containing two muddy football boots. How could he have forgotten it?

Pushing the gate shut, Banksie hurried

down the path at the side of the ho
would still be in the kitchen where he'c
five minutes ago, dunking biscuits in t

Voices. Banksie pressed his ear aga
door. Mac and his mum – from the tone
voices, they were having an argument.

Creeping round the back of the
Banksie peeped through the kitchen w
His bag was just where he'd left it, und
table. Mac was seated. Mrs MacBride l
against the worktop, still dressed in the s
dark office suit she'd turned up to watc
match in. A few parents had come at the e
the game to pick up their offspring, but
MacBride had been there throughout.
shook her head. 'Just like your father was,
said, stubbing out her cigarette.

Mac glared. *'How* am I?'

'Too easy-going.'

'You always say that!'

'Well it's true.'

'No one else thinks so.'

'Then they don't know you,' said
MacBride. 'You're soft: you've no very
drive to get *on* in the world.'

Banksie bit a nail.

Mac glowered at his mum. 'That's not

'How not?'

'The football trials were only last wee

you to make something of yourself. And I know you have it in you to do so. You're *not* your father. I say those things about you, because I want to make sure you don't turn out like him.'

Banksie chewed the last remaining shreds of thumb nail. Perhaps Mac's mum was always like this at home? That would explain why he was so pushy.

'You still have all your opportunities ahead of you,' said Mrs MacBride, 'and I'm *determined* you won't waste them.'

Mac's head had dropped. 'I don't want to be a disappointment to you,' he croaked.

'Then *don't* be.' Mrs MacBride touched the back of his neck. 'Show me what you're made of, what you're *really* made of. Be a *man*.'

Sliding away from the window, Banksie tiptoed round the side of the house and hurried towards the street. No way was he knocking now. The boots would have to spend the night under their table.

6
HILL

St Dunstan's school stood on high ground. The quiet, tree-lined street ran up to the main road with its few shops. A short distance around the corner, the main road began its long, steep descent beside the heath. The last shop was Sid's Newsagents. There were bus stops just beyond and a couple of benches, from where people gazed out over the city panorama.

Banksie and Mac made their way along the high street.

'Dunk's skivvies.' Mac drained his Coke can and crushed it in his hand. 'That's what Powelly's asking us to be.' He flung the can at a roadside bin. Bouncing off the rim, it clattered along the pavement. A smartly dressed woman side-stepped, frowning disapprovingly. Mac booted it with a vengeance.

'You don't think you might be overreacting?'

said Banksie. Mac seemed determined to grumble about the previous day's friendly at every opportunity.

Mac snorted. 'As soon as I showed initiative, Powell slapped me down.' He stomped the can with his heel. 'What's the point?'

'It *was* our first game,' said Banksie. 'We knew the score. Give Powelly a chance – he *is* the man in charge.'

'Oh, how could I forget,' said Mac, 'and Dunk's so brilliant. Dunk's so *gifted*. Dunk's so blinking marvellous.'

'Come on!' chuckled Banksie. 'We made a good impression. Not one of those goals would have been scored without us. Powelly likes you. He had nothing but praise for us after the match.'

Mac scowled. 'But there could so easily have been more, if it hadn't been for his stupid insistence we always give the ball to Dunk.'

'Powell's got his plans,' said Banksie, 'and his way of doing things. What's important is that we did what we were asked, and did it well.'

Mac grunted. 'Yeah, I suppose we played all right on the whole.'

'More than all right.'

Mac managed a smile. 'MacB and Banksie. Banksie and MacB!'

'The big question now,' said Banksie, 'is do we get to keep our places?'

Mac laughed. 'No two ways about it, mate!'

'You're very certain,' said Banksie, 'all of a sudden.'

Mac widened his eyes. 'The prophesy,' he chuckled.

Krrrrrrrrrr.

As the two boys span round, Dunk skidded his bike to a stop against the curb. 'Guys!' He grinned. 'On your way to Sid's?'

'Yup.' Banksie nodded.

'Great minds think alike.' Dunk jerked his front wheel up the kerb. 'Excellent result yesterday. Powell's well pleased. You two slogged your guts out.' Standing on the pedals, he nosed the bike between them.

'We were just talking about you,' said Mac, 'as it happens.'

'Nothing good I hope.'

'Four quality goals!' said Mac. 'What could be bad about that, first game of the season.'

'A great team effort,' Dunk nodded. 'With you two feeding through the excellent passes, over and over, it was hard to go wrong. You worked like dogs.'

'You're too modest,' said Mac. 'Come on, you don't get to be solo striker and team captain without being pretty special.'

Dunk laughed and shook his head. Yanking his bike up into a wheelie, he pedalled ahead, then braked.

Mac and Banksie caught up.

'There's Mel and Don.' Dunk nodded across the street. 'I should go and say hello. Maybe see you in Sid's.'

Mac and Banksie watched him weave his way through the traffic.

'You've changed your tune!' chuckled Banksie.

'What you talking about?'

'"Four quality goals,"' said Banksie, imitating his friend. '"You're too modest."'

'Dunk was complimentary about you and me.'

'But *he* means it.'

'And I don't?'

'Do you?'

Mac shrugged and grinned. 'I'm off home, mate. Got no money for Sid's today. Catch you later.'

'What was all that about?' Jamming another wine gum into his cheek, Banksie followed Dunk round the side of the shop to where his bike was locked.

There had been an ugly moment in the newsagents. Mel, Don and some other boys had followed Dunk inside; Mel and Don had shouted abuse. Dunk had tried to ignore them, but they had only got louder. They had started pushing and shoving. Sid had warned them, then threatened to call the police when they carried on. Only when he'd picked up the phone and dialled, had they finally cleared off.

'They think it's down to me,' said Dunk, 'who gets in the team and who doesn't.' He shoved the big metal lock into its bracket under the crossbar. 'They're saying I've been disloyal because you and Mac got a trial game. They're accusing me of not doing enough to keep them in the team!'

'That's stupid,' said Banksie. 'It's not up to you.'

Dunk nodded. 'Kind of understandable though.' Slotting bike lights into front and rear brackets, he switched them on to check the batteries. 'It's nothing definite, OK, but from what Powelly's told me, you and Mac are favourites to start Saturday's league opener.'

'Yeah?' Banksie heard the excitement in his own voice. He jerked his thumb towards the shop. 'You told *them* that too?'

Dunk nodded.

'No wonder they were narked!'

'I thought I should at least warn them of the

possibility,' said Dunk. 'Guess I judged it wrong!'

The two boys made their way along the pavement. Light was fading, colour draining from the world. Only pastel shades and grey remained. The steep sweep of the hill dropped away to the city below, houses one side, darkening heath the other. Sparkling in the distance, a string of tiny jewels heralded lighting-up time. Cars had begun to switch on headlights.

'I should scoot,' said Dunk. He patted the crossbar. 'I'd offer you a lift, but I ought to get a move on.' He inclined his head. 'And on this road it's a little dangerous.'

'No problem,' said Banksie. 'I'm cutting across the heath anyway. It won't take me long.'

'Laters, then.'

'Yeah, laters.'

Pushing off from the pavement, Dunk waved and bent low over the handlebars. Banksie watched as he gathered speed on the gradient. Briefly, comically, Dunk lifted his legs out to both sides, freewheeling. Then he vanished into the traffic.

Banksie turned to set off across the heath.

An instant later, he was spinning back towards the road. Somehow he already recognized the stomach-churning sound. As he ran, follow-on noises floated up the hill. A crunch, the tinkle of glass, another crunch. *Another* crunch.

A terrible silence.

His feet thumped on the pavement.

And then screaming. He thought it was a siren at first. *How could it be?* There *was* a siren somewhere below in the city, dashing to some other emergency, but the louder, nearer sound was screaming – real and human. A woman's wail, rising into the air.

The traffic was stationary. People were craning their necks, opening doors, some even climbing out as he ran by, down the hill. Someone called out, 'I'm through to emergency services . . . what's the name of this road?' The grey evening light seemed to Banksie, to be dimming by the second, darkening as he descended. The screaming had stopped.

A large dark shape, an estate car, blocked the pavement at an absurd angle, its front end propped jauntily against a lamp post. A couple were sitting on the ground beside it, the man with his arm around the woman, comforting her. Banksie heard himself ask: 'Were you screaming?' The woman and man shook their heads.

He ran on, round the car, past other cars in odd positions, past dazed-looking people holding each other, comforting each other, past two cars concertinaed nose to nose.

Tick . . . tick . . . tick.

Banksie jerked round. A flicker of wheel spokes, still gently turning in the dying light. A twisted bike frame, its back broken beneath a car.

Just beyond, standing on the grass, a man held a woman. Banksie recognized the voice from the screaming. 'He just crashed into me,' the woman sobbed, 'he just *flew through the air* and smashed into me!'

At their feet, another man crouched on the ground beside a body. Two twisted legs, a familiar face . . . two terrified eyes.

Banksie knelt. Touched blood.

Dunk's eyes fluttered shut.

7
BLOOD

The door opened half way. Shanice's eyes narrowed. 'Yes . . .?'

'Miss Banks?'

She nodded. 'What's wrong?'

'I'm WPC Quinley and this is PC Redfern, my colleague. Would either of your parents be at home?'

'Why?' Shanice stepped out on to the mat. 'What's happened?'

Banksie felt himself being pushed, very gently, forwards.

Shanice gave a little start.

'It's OK.' The policewoman's voice softened a touch. 'Your brother isn't hurt.'

Shanice frowned. 'Is he in trouble?'

'No,' said the policewoman, 'but probably in shock. There's been a traffic accident, quite a serious one, I'm afraid. A boy from your brother's school was hit by a car . . .'

Shanice's hand shot to her mouth. 'Oh my God!'

The policeman nodded. 'I'm afraid the boy appears to have been quite badly injured. Your brother was one of the first on the scene. He waited with him till the emergency services arrived. He's been very brave.'

Shanice grabbed her brother's hand. 'You OK?'

Banksie nodded.

She squeezed his fingers. 'Was it someone –'

'Dunk.'

'Oh *no* . . .' Shanice hugged him. 'No. How awful!'

'What about your parents?' said the policewoman. 'Are they likely to be home soon?'

Shanice shrugged. 'It's mum's yoga night – she goes straight from work. Dad always works late. Don't worry, I can take care of my brother.'

'You're sure you'll be all right?'

Shanice nodded.

'OK.' The policewoman smiled. 'In our experience, nothing beats a nice cup of tea.'

The policeman nodded. 'With a couple of extra sugars.' He winked and turned. The policewoman gave a little wave.

Shanice pushed the door closed. 'Right then.' She sighed. 'Come and sit down. I'll make you a lovely cuppa.'

'I'm fine,' muttered Banksie. 'You don't have to.'

'You don't *sound* fine,' said Shanice. 'Your voice is as flat as a pancake. A cup of tea's no trouble. Come on.' She tugged at his blazer. 'Look at you! There's *blood* all over your shirt!'

'Dunk was bleeding.' Banksie brushed her hand away. 'It's OK. I'm all right.' He pushed past her. 'I'm going round to Mac's.'

'What!'

Banksie opened the door. 'I'm fine.'

'Don't be stupid!' Shanice slammed the door shut. 'You're in shock.'

'I need to see him,' said Banksie. 'It's only a short walk.'

'What's so important?'

'He's my mate.' Banksie shrugged. A sense of foreboding had been gnawing at him since the accident. It wasn't something he could explain to Shanice. 'He was with me and Dunk just before it happened.'

'And?'

'I ought to let him know.'

'You could call,' said Shanice.

'Uh-uh.' Banksie shook his head and snapped back the latch. For reasons he couldn't fathom, the fortune-teller's prophesy kept coming to mind. And Mrs MacBride shouting at Mac. 'I have to see him. Now.'

'OK.' Shanice stopped the door with her foot. 'But if you won't wait till Mum or Dad gets home, I'm coming too.'

'What!' Banksie scowled. 'No way!' He yanked the door hard.

'Sorry!' Shanice's foot held firm. 'But I told the police I'd look after you, remember?' She grinned. 'Wherever you go, *I* go.'

Mac grinned out into the dark. 'Hey, Banksie.' The smile evaporated. 'You look *terrible*!' He grunted, spotting Shanice. 'What's *she* doing here?'

'I'm looking after him,' said Shanice. 'He's had a very nasty experience. He insisted on coming round to tell you about it. God knows why.'

Mac stared at his friend. Suddenly, both hands shot up to his face. 'Blood!' he gasped. 'Are you OK?'

Banksie nodded. 'It's not mine.' He opened his blazer to show Mac the extent of the blood stains.

Mac caught his breath. '*Ssshhh . . . sugar!*'

'It's Dunk's,' said Banksie.

'*What!*' Mac blanched.

'There was an accident.'

Mac shook his head. 'But . . . so much blood?'

'He got hit by a car,' said Banksie.

'That's terrible,' said Mac. 'What happened?'

'He didn't actually see the accident,' said Shanice.

'But you saw Dunk?' said Mac.

Banksie nodded.

'Is he going to be OK?'

'I don't know.' There was a quiver in Banksie's voice. 'It was a pile-up – six or seven cars . . .'

'Six or seven!' Mac's eyes looked like they might pop from their sockets.

'Dunk lost a lot of blood,' said Banksie. 'I know that much. He was unconscious. I stayed with him till the ambulance arrived. Onc leg –' he shuddered, seeing it all again – 'one leg was definitely broken. The paramedic told me to ring the hospital later.'

'What about the other people,' said Shanice, 'the people in the cars?'

'I don't know.' Banksie shook his head. 'I saw someone go off in another ambulance.'

Mac's mouth hung open. 'I can't believe it.'

'It was really . . . *scary*,' gasped Banksie. He covered his face with his hands to hide the tears.

'We'll call the hospital when we get home,' said Shanice. Gently, she slipped an arm round him. 'Come on, we should go. Mum'll be worried if she finds we're not there.'

'Poor old Dunk . . .' Mac was still shaking his head. 'Such bad luck. I can't believe it.'

8

FALLOUT

'OK,' said Mr Powell, 'that's it for the time being. Gather round and make yourselves comfortable. Team talk.'

Red faced, sweating and panting, boys grunted with relief and flopped to the ground. Banksie picked a spot next to Mac.

'That was too hard, sir!'

'I won't be able to move for a week, sir!'

Mr Powell tutted and shook his head. For well over an hour, he had put them through their paces. The training session had started with a 'warm-up' jog, twice round the playing field, led by himself. Then, he had lined them up and put them through sets of his 'killer callisthenics' – press-ups, sit-ups, star jumps, squats and crunches.

Following this, in pairs, they had run through assorted ball-skills routines – working on heading, dribbling, shooting and tackling.

But Mr Powell had saved his favourite torture for last – interval sprints, from the centre to the eighteen-yard line, against the stopwatch, with the briefest of recovery times. That had been the real killer.

'As all of you have no doubt heard,' said Mr Powell, 'on Monday, Duncan King was seriously injured – a road accident on his way home from school.'

Without looking up, Banksie sensed the heads turning. Over the last few days he had grown used to everyone's curiosity and questions. School had been buzzing with the news. Those that hadn't known him from Adam before, recognized him now; everybody knew about his involvement. In classrooms and corridors, the dinner hall and the school yard, the whispers and glances had spread like wildfire. It was the first time in his life he had been such an object of interest. On balance, he didn't much like it.

'I spoke to the hospital this lunch time,' said Mr Powell. 'Duncan has two broken legs, torn ligaments, a broken arm, several cracked ribs and a punctured lung.' He sighed wearily and shook his head. 'Thankfully, he has now regained consciousness. But I think it's safe to assume he won't be taking part in any fixtures for the foreseeable future.'

Heads bowed.

'So, that has left me with a rather difficult decision . . .' Mr Powell looked up from his clipboard. 'Who do I put up front?'

Banksie glanced. Mac's green eyes had narrowed to dagger points. At the receiving end of the stare, Don and Mel glared back.

'My decision is bound to disappoint some and please others,' continued Mr Powell. 'In view of the circumstances, please receive it with magnanimity.'

Banksie held his breath. The knuckles of his hands were clenched white around his knees.

'This Saturday we'll be playing a four-four-two formation, with Banks and MacB our paired strikers.'

Don's jaw dropped; Mel shook his head slowly and stared at the ground.

Mac turned to Banksie and grinned.

'The back row,' continued Mr Powell, 'remains the same. But as far as the midfield are concerned – I want Cappri and Thomas to cover the centre behind MacB and Banks. With all his experience, I think Thomas is the logical choice for captain.'

There were a few small cheers, some grunts and murmurs. Mel grinned two rows of gleaming white teeth. Don smiled smugly at his side.

'Eaton,' said Mr Powell, 'you will take the

right wing. Wallace, the left. The names of the full squad will be posted on the notice board in the main hall entrance, by the start of school tomorrow.' He glanced at his watch. 'Right! Just time for a gentle warm down and stretch. What d'you say – a couple more times round the field?'

The groans of protest were pitiful.

'On your feet!'

'Third turning on the left.'

Following the nurse's directions, Mac and Banksie marched swiftly down the corridor. They paused at the ward entrance.

Banksie stared – Mac looked pale and queasy. 'You sure you're all right?'

'I told you,' said Mac, 'hospitals make me nervous. It's the smell. This is a quick visit, right?'

Banksie nodded.

The nurse pointed them to the far end of the ward. Medical machinery and paraphernalia cluttered the space around the bed.

Dunk's eyes followed the two boys as they approached; the head didn't turn, but the lips moved. A stylishly dressed woman rose to her feet. She was tall and pretty, but there were grey-blue crescents of weariness beneath the kind eyes.

'I'm Katherine King.' There was a trace of American accent. She turned to Banksie. 'You're the boy who stayed with my son till the ambulance arrived?'

Banksie nodded.

Tears welled. She embraced him in an awkward half hug. 'We're so grateful . . .' Turning, she held out her hand to Mac. 'You don't look well.'

'It's hospitals,' Mac scowled, 'they don't agree with me.'

Mrs King shrugged. 'Duncan tires very easily at the moment.' She gestured to the man and two girls seated around the bed. 'My husband and daughters,' said Mrs King. 'We'll go for a little stretch and find ourselves a cup of tea.'

Dunk smiled weakly as the two friends sat. 'Thanks . . .' His voice rasped, barely a whisper. 'Thanks, Banksie.'

Banksie shrugged. 'How are you?' He grinned. 'Bit of a stupid question I know, but . . .'

Dunk smiled again and, with his eyes, indicated the bandaging around his chest. He raised an eyebrow. 'Can't laugh . . .' His eyes flickered to his two legs – suspended above the bed in plaster casts. His gaze travelled up to his plaster-casted arm, across to the tubes entering his body via his hand and then, behind the drips, to the various items of monitoring equipment. 'Oops!'

Banksie grinned. 'Oops!'

'Sorry.' Dunk's eyes twinkled. 'Won't be able to make the match, Saturday.'

Mac and Banksie laughed.

'Don't worry,' said Mac, 'Banksie and me'll take care of things up front.'

Dunk gave a slight nod. He tried to smile. His chest heaved and shuddered; his eyes fluttered and closed.

Banksie leant forward. 'You all right?'

The eyelids lifted heavily. 'Sorry . . .' Dunk frowned and swallowed. '. . . tired.'

'D'you want to sleep?' said Banksie.

'No . . .' Dunk coughed to clear his throat, but his voice remained a hoarse whisper. 'It was no accident.'

'Sorry?' said Banksie. 'No accident? You mean *your* accident?'

Eyes drooping, Dunk grunted.

Mac leant close. 'You think the driver deliberately crashed into you?'

'No.' Dunk's eyes fluttered, his head slumped.

Banksie and Mac exchanged glances across the bed.

'Duncan talked to the police this morning . . .'

The two boys swivelled. Mrs King had returned, alone.

'He told them he believed his bike might have been sabotaged.'

'*Sabotaged?*'

Mrs King nodded. 'It was the first thing he said when he recovered consciousness. I thought perhaps he was delirious, but –' she shrugged – 'the police appear to be taking his claim seriously. They went off right away, to examine the wreck of his bike.'

'Did they find anything?' said Mac.

'We're still waiting to hear,' said Mrs King. 'Oh, excuse me a moment.'

The nurse beckoned from the ward entrance.

Dunk made a coughing sort of sound. His eyes fluttered and opened again. When Mrs King returned, she was accompanied by the nurse and two men.

'Five minutes,' said the nurse, addressing them all. 'It's essential he gets his rest.'

Mrs King turned to the boys. 'This is Detective Sergeant Cosgrove,' she said, indicating the fatter and balder of the two men. His eyes were hidden behind dark glasses, his suit was baggy and tired looking.

'Hello, boys.' He nodded.

His partner was younger and slimmer.

Instead of a suit, he wore jeans, trainers and a jacket. 'Detective Steve Nichols,' he said.

Mac threw Banksie a look. 'We should be going,' he said.

'Don't be silly!' said Mrs King. She turned to the detectives. 'These two boys are friends of Duncan's from school.' She nodded to Banksie. 'This is the boy who waited with my son till the ambulance arrived.'

'Good man,' said Cosgrove. He grasped Banksie's hand and shook it firmly. 'Well played, son.'

Banksie blushed.

The big man squeezed past the apparatus holding the tubes which flowed into Dunk's hand. 'How's the patient?' He leaned close. 'Feeling up to a little chat?'

Dunk blinked and managed a tilt of his head. 'Uh-huh,' he rasped.

'That's my boy!' Cosgrove peered over his dark glasses at his partner. 'How, I'd like to know, does a young man go through all this –' he indicated the drips and the plaster casts – 'land on his bonce, get knocked out for a couple of days, then wake up with a completely spot-on hunch about sabotage?'

Dunk's eyes lit up. 'You found it?'

'You didn't sabotage your own bike, now, did you, son?'

Dunk's face darkened. 'No!' he blurted. He began coughing. 'I did not!'

'Please!' Mrs King stroked her son's fingers. 'You mustn't upset him, Mr Cosgrove.'

'I'm sorry . . . I'm sorry, son,' said Cosgrove. '*I* know you never. But, under the circumstances, I have to ask.'

'Just part of the routine,' added Nichols. He held up a small cellophane bag. 'The cause of all our grief.'

Banksie stared at the contents – a twisted piece of wire.

Cosgrove shook his head, wearily. 'Almost certainly a paperclip.' He sighed. 'Just as you suspected: the derailleur jammed.' He tapped the bag. 'We found this little fella wrapped tightly round the chain.'

'Simple,' said Nichols. 'But – travelling at speed, downhill – *deadly*.'

'Have you found fingerprints?' asked Mrs King.

Cosgrove chuckled. 'We could try dusting the bike, I suppose.' He pointed to the bag. 'But we're not going to get anything off of *that*.' He sighed and rubbed the bridge of his nose.

'This is a serious crime,' said Nichols.

Cosgrove nodded. 'Very serious. Duncan here is lucky to be alive.'

Banksie watched Dunk's eyelids droop and close.

'Poor darling,' whispered Mrs King.

'Whoever did this,' said Nichols, 'has to be caught.'

'That's right,' said Cosgrove. 'Could have been a foolish prank, or someone with a grudge. Either way, we need to find them.'

'Excuse me.' The nurse reappeared, frowning and tapping her watch.

'Of course,' said Cosgrove, glancing at Dunk. 'The poor boy's asleep anyway.' He patted Banksie, nodded to Mac. 'We'll be visiting your school. If either of you hears anything, you be sure to let us know.'

9

STRIKERS

It hadn't been a good week for the team's morale. Dunk's 'accident' had been followed by a lurking police presence at school – the investigation. Accounts of the incident in the newsagents had become widespread, rumours rife. It had all become too much for Don and Mel; finally losing patience with the whispers and glances, they had lashed out. Pranett, an annoying year-sixer, had caught the full force. He'd been sent home with a nose bleed, two black eyes and a chipped tooth. Don and Mel had been suspended. They would *not* be playing.

In a cramped, smelly dressing room with only one light, Mr Powell was doing his best to reorganize the team and raise spirits. But it was uphill all the way.

Mac was one of the more buoyant. 'So what are this lot *like*?' he asked.

Mr Powell dangled a seriously soiled sock from his finger tips. 'If these facilities are anything to go by – dishevelled and disorganized.'

'And stinking too, sir?'

Mr Powell lifted the sock at a distance from his nose and sniffed, gingerly. 'Not a little!'

Boys laughed, in spite of the fetid air. Wags pretended to choke.

'I wouldn't want us to get too complacent,' said Mr Powell, 'Haddon High's own changing room is probably five star.' He attempted to jam the door open. 'When you're ready, out you go. There's no point staying in here longer than necessary.'

As boys finished changing and left the room, Mr Powell ticked them off, one by one, on his clipboard.

Banksie was first out. Over by the pitch, among a crowd of mostly opposition supporters, he spotted Mrs MacBride sipping from a steaming cup. No distance was too far for her to travel, she had made it to each game. She waved and smiled. Testing the grass for dryness, Banksie sat and inhaled deeply through his nostrils. 'Fresh air,' he gasped, 'at last!'

'In there's a blinkin' danger to health.' Jake 'Big Hands' Gregg, the team's goalie, paused panting in the doorway. 'It ought to be fumigated.'

Mr Powell nodded.

'*Bombed* more like!' Mac tried in vain to squeeze past Gregg's large frame. 'Let me out!' he gasped, feigning suffocation. 'I'm gagging.' When Gregg obliged, Mac staggered forward to sniff the clean air. 'Ahh . . . beautiful!'

Nathan Woddis trotted out behind. Compact body, frowning face. 'I reckon they put us in there to poison us,' he grunted, 'but it ain't gonna work!'

Mr Powell checked his list. 'You'll be playing at left-back. I'm sticking Sonny Patel on the outside.'

'Suits me.'

Sonny's smiling face appeared at the door. 'And me!'

Mr Powell waved him out. 'Come on, the rest of you – let's have you!'

Honey-skinned Anton Ridley came next, locks tied back in a ponytail.

'You would have been starting on the bench,' said Mr Powell, 'but due to our unfortunate circumstances, you'll be taking the place of Melvin Thomas.'

Ridley nodded and sat. Tall Jamie Wallace sat down beside him.

'Left-wing,' said Mr Powell. 'I'm expecting

great things from you, Wallace. Young Harry was waiting to jump in your boots, but he now has to cover for Cappri. So don't let me down.'

Harry Oliver and Terry Eaton, the two quiet members of the squad, followed each other out. Little Harry, light on his feet and a ferocious tackler. Gangly, greasy-haired Terry, the other winger.

Mr Powell nodded to Terry and waved him to join the others. 'Harry,' he said, 'it's Cappri's boots you'll be filling today, not Wallace's.'

Harry shrugged and nodded.

At the other end of the pavilion, the Haddon High players began to file out.

'Who does that leave . . .?' Mr Powell leant inside the dressing room. 'McAllister, right-back and . . . Charlie Cook, wing-back on the right. Come on, you two! Get a move on or they'll be starting without us.' Clapping his hands he turned and set off towards the pitch.

McAllister's frame filled the doorway. 'Sir?'

'What is it, McA?'

'With Thomas not being here, sir, we don't have a captain.'

'Didn't I say?' Mr Powell tutted. 'With all this disruption I'm losing my marbles.' He peered at his clipboard. 'Thank you for reminding me, McA. In Thomas's absence, I'm nominating MacB to take charge on pitch.'

'Me, sir?' Mac stopped in his tracks. 'Team captain, sir?' His eyes seemed momentarily to glaze.

'You're up to the job aren't you, MacB?'

'Yes, sir!' Mac nodded vigorously. 'You bet!'

'Good.' Mr Powell smiled. 'Your priority is still goals. Being captain mustn't distract you.'

'No, sir.'

As the team jogged their way towards the pitch, Mac made his way towards the front of the pack.

Banksie nudged him as he overtook. 'Nice one!'

Mac winked. Grinning, he made a discreet, triumphant fist, then spurted forward, head held high, leading the team to the centre.

Cheers rose above the polite applause of opposition players and supporters. Banksie scanned the faces, certain Mac's mum would be punching the air in celebration of her son's achievement. But the enthusiastic sounds belonged to someone else. Mrs MacBride stood completely still on the edge of the crowd, smiling in silence.

The first half was, on the face of it, nothing to write home about. But, given that they were fielding a side who had never all played together, with a captain new to the team *and* the role, St Dunstan's had not done too badly to be 2–1 down.

Mr Powell's half-time talk was characterized by moderate praise and muscular encouragement. In particular, for the determined efforts of Mac and Banksie up front. Haddon's goalie had proved himself more competent than most in keeping out so many shots. A little something extra was needed. And, scrambling to their feet for the start of the second half, St Dunstan's attack force knew they had to find it.

'We can do it!' Mac was all fired up. 'The first half was our warm up – we were busy trying to get a feel for each other, yeah?'

Oliver, Ridley and Wallace nodded. Eaton grunted.

'Like Powelly says, now we're ready to up the tempo.' Mac made a fist. 'Smart and fast – that's how we need to play. Let's snatch this game from them.'

The boys dispersed to their positions. 'Three goals in the first half,' yelled Mr Powell from the touchline. He thrust three fingers aloft. 'I want three in the second – all of them *ours*.'

The whistle blew. Banksie received the short pass from Mac, tapped it back to Oliver and moved on, looking for space. As the first red shirts surged wildly over the centre line, St

Dunstan's began a steady advance. But Oliver hung back, waiting for the right moment.

Banksie called for the ball. Mac too.

Oliver's dummy to Wallace threw two of the charging Haddons the wrong way. He twisted and made a long pass out to the right. Eaton streaked on to the ball and began accelerating up the wing. Suddenly, St Dunstan's were on the warpath.

Now Banksie sprinted alongside his captain. They and their back-up were all well inside Haddon's territory. Haddon had dangerously overreached themselves, they had missed the trick and were going to get *burned*.

'It doesn't take three to tackle him!' Haddon's keeper yelled furiously, desperate to shore up his defence. 'Who's covering the *centre*?'

But it was too late. Already inside the penalty area, Mac and Banksie had unstoppable momentum.

Eaton's cross came in high. Panicking defenders jumped early and short. Mac leapt, stretching into the air; his brow made contact, he nudged the ball down across the goal.

Banksie flung himself, feet first. He clipped the ball just inside the post and followed through, bum-sliding gracefully under the back of the net.

'Yes!'

His first goal for St Dunstan's! *Yes!* Banksie skipped . . . cartwheeled and . . . *back-flipped*! Suddenly, his teammates were all around him, hugging him and patting him, some of them trying to jump on him.

'Neat.' Mac nodded curtly. 'Come on, lads. Back to position. Let's keep our minds on the game.'

That first goal, the equaliser at the start of the half had, apparently, given Haddon Hall a fright. From then on in, they'd chucked everything they'd got into derailing St Dunstan's assaults. Scarcely venturing over the centre line, the Haddon boys had managed to block every St Dunstan's initiative.

Frustration was etched deep on Mac's brow, increasing recklessness undermined his moves. Banksie knew his mate too well – behind his terse, tight-lipped commands lay fury at *him*, for having matched his first goal. It was essential St Dunstan's should win. But more importantly, Mac *had to be* top goal scorer. The streak that couldn't bear to be beaten, drove him on, desperately on.

And it was Mac's second goal that finally broke the impasse; five minutes from the end, putting St Dunstan's into the lead. The atmosphere became electric.

'Come on, you Reds!' chanted Haddon Hall's supporters, with renewed vigour and volume. 'Come *on*! Come *on*! Come *on*, you REDS!'

'No resting on laurels,' yelled Mac.

'That's right, MacB!' Mr Powell cupped his hands to make himself heard. *'One more GOAL.'*

'Come on, St Dunstan's!' Heavily outnumbered, the St Dunstan's supporters struck up a chant to counter their rivals. 'St Dunstan's, St Dunstan's, *one more goal*! St Dunstan's, St Dunstan's, *one more goal*!'

'Don't stop now!' A single shrill voice cut across the shouts and chants. 'One more goal, MacB! A *hat-trick*, MacB! Come on – *we want a hat-trick*!' Mrs MacBride strode along the Haddon goal line, defying the home crowd.

At the whistle, Mac led the charge. Banksie followed close on his heels, with the midfield fanning out behind. Haddon passed back, passed across, then further back, desperate to maintain possession.

'Go on, St Dunstan's!'

'Go for it, MacB!'

Mac harried Haddon's captain. The captain passed the ball wide.

'Come on, the REDS!'

Banksie bore down on the wing-back, sliding in to block his pass. The deflected ball shot into touch off the Haddon player's ankle. Banksie span. Players from both sides had their hands in the air, but the vigilant ref was signalling in St Dunstan's favour.

'Come on!' yelled Mac, 'I want *everyone* forward!'

Banksie looked for space. As Wallace's throw soared through the air, he jumped, caught the ball on his chest and hit the ground twisting.

Mac whistled from the crowded goal area.

Banksie volleyed. The ball rebounded off a charging defender. Chipping it straight to Mac, he ran in.

Mac's shot was a rocket, but straight at the keeper. Ricocheting upwards, the ball flew out off the crossbar.

Red shirts threw themselves left, right and centre. Wallace went down. Little Harry Oliver got a foot to it. From out of nowhere, Nat Woddis tried a flying dive. The ball cannoned off a defender and bounced to Banksie.

'Banksie!'

Banksie skipped a sliding tackle, swerved left and right, and once more pushed it through – a perfect pass – to his captain.

Mac's right leg swung down with deadly accuracy. The keeper dived. But the ball arced into the net.

'Goal!'

The ref blew his whistle. Then, checking his watch, blew twice more.

It was over.

10

CORROBORATION

Banksie knocked on the door. It was ajar. He pushed.

'Come in!' DS Cosgrove's voice boomed around the empty classroom. He was half sitting, half leaning on the corner of the teacher's desk. Detective Nichols was at the back of the classroom, gazing at projects on the wall.

'Ah . . .' Cosgrove held out his hand and smiled warmly. The spectacles had lost their darkness and behind them his eyes twinkled. 'Our man of the moment. Sorry to drag you away from your lesson. Anything interesting?'

Banksie shrugged. 'Only English . . . we're doing Shakespeare.'

Cosgrove chuckled. 'Well, I won't keep you long . . . have a seat.'

Banksie hopped up on to one of the front row of desks.

'As you know, Detective Nichols and I have

been talking to a lot of boys over the last week, trying to build up a picture of what goes on in the school: who knows who, who's mates with who, who *doesn't* like who and so on.'

Banksie swung his dangling legs back and forth, under the desk.

'Now, if memory serves me right –' Cosgrove rummaged through a pile of papers beside him on the desk – 'last time we spoke, you told us that, prior to the argument in the newsagents –' he scanned a page of spidery scrawl – 'where are we? Ah, yes . . . you and your friend MacBride had been walking together up the high street?'

'Yep.' Banksie nodded. 'That's right.'

'I'm trying to get a better idea of who was in the area around the time things were happening,' said Cosgrove, 'for corroboration purposes. Now, how long would you say it takes to walk from here to Sid's? Twenty minutes?'

'Yeah, probably about that,' said Banksie. 'We don't tend to rush.'

Cosgrove smiled. 'And MacBride, you say, walked with you most of the way.'

'Practically all the way. He didn't have any money, so he didn't want to go to the newsagents.'

'Uh-huh . . .' Cosgrove rifled through his

papers again. He tutted, shook his head and scribbled a short note on another piece of paper. 'Right,' he said finally, 'thank you. I think that's all I needed. Better get back to your English.' He glanced at his watch. 'Not much left I'm afraid!'

Mac and Banksie shuffled through the throng, funnelling towards the school doors.

'So did they want to know more about Don and Mel?' asked Mac.

'Nope,' said Banksie. 'They asked about me and you. You mostly.'

'Me?' Mac stumbled as the swing door caught him off balance. 'How d'you mean *me*? What did you tell them?'

'Nothing really.' Banksie shrugged. 'They just wanted to know about the day of Dunk's accident – how far we walked together, after school.'

Mac stared.

'What's up?' said Banksie. 'You OK?'

Mac frowned.

'You all right?' said Banksie. 'You've gone a bit pale.'

Mac rubbed his thigh. 'That door whacked me, right on the side.'

'Probably gave you a dead leg.'

Mac puffed hard a couple of times. 'I'm OK.'

Slowly, the two boys made their way across the yard. At the gates, Mac seemed surprised to see his mother.

'Ah!' Mrs MacBride dropped her cigarette and ground it under her shoe. 'The footballing hero!' She smiled and waved. 'And, of course, his heroic friend.'

Standing beside her car, were two familiar figures.

'I've just met your detectives,' said Mrs MacBride.

Cosgrove and Nichols nodded.

Banksie glanced at Mac. He still looked pale.

'We were waiting to have a word,' said Cosgrove. 'But then your mother introduced herself. And she seems to have answered all our queries.' He glanced at his partner.

Nichols nodded. 'Cleared up everything.'

'Honestly! What a dope!' Mrs MacBride's eyes narrowed on her son. 'Telling the detectives I picked you up from school, the day of Duncan's horrible accident.'

Banksie felt the hairs on the back of his neck prickle.

'I . . .' Mac looked sheepish. 'I can't have been thinking . . .'

Mrs MacBride scowled. 'They're conducting an *investigation,* darling. You have to give precise information. It's important.'

'Your mother explained,' said Cosgrove, 'she spotted you in the high street and gave you a lift home.'

Mac nodded. 'Yeah . . . er, Banksie had just crossed the road.' He glanced at his mother. 'He'd gone to the newsagents with Dunk. I was heading for the heath.'

Banksie studied his friend's face. Why then, had Mac told them he'd been picked up from school? He had *lied*.

'Your mother's also given us some very useful extra information,' said Cosgrove.

'I told you to tell the detectives *everything*.' Mrs MacBride ruffled her son's hair. 'I don't know what comes over you sometimes.'

'Two boys,' said Cosgrove, lowering his voice. He stepped closer. 'Your mother said that when you and she were sitting in the traffic, you noticed two boys loitering round the side of Sid's newsagents?'

Banksie's heart raced. Mac had never mentioned a word of this.

Mac glanced at his mother and nodded.

'Boys you recognized?' said Cosgrove.

Mac nodded again.

'Who would they have been, then?'

Mac looked at the ground. 'Don and Mel,' he croaked.

Banksie stared in disbelief. Why would Mac

have kept *this* a secret? Perhaps he was worried that because of their rivalry he'd not be believed?

'I didn't quite catch that,' said Cosgrove.

Mac coughed to clear his throat. 'Donatello Cappri and Melvin Thomas.'

'Thank you.' Cosgrove gave Mac a small pat on the shoulder. Turning to Mrs MacBride, he sighed and held out his hand. 'And thank you. You've been a tremendous help.'

'You're more than welcome,' said Mrs MacBride. 'I'm glad to be of assistance under such awful circumstances.'

11

FOUL

'Birnam Wood, Birnam Wood – we're going to win the cup!'

Trying not to look too pleased with himself, Banksie sat in the circle with his gloomy teammates, rubbing bumps and bruises. He had scored *both* goals – the first: a spectacular solo run through the defence, the second: a header from a corner. Both goals!

Mr Powell paced back and forth. 'We knew they were going to be a difficult side. But frankly, I'm gobsmacked by their conduct. They should be ashamed. As for the ref . . .'

Banksie hurled a clod of mud and grass at the goal post. If Birnam hadn't been such foulers and the ref so useless, his two goals would have put St Dunstan's ahead. But there had been a raft of questionable decisions and now they were 2–3 behind. 'The ref is blind,' he grunted, 'or he's an idiot.'

'Perhaps he's just intimidated by the home crowd,' said Gregg. 'They're loud enough!'

'Maybe,' sneered Mac, 'he's taking backhanders from Birnam.' He jabbed a finger in the direction of the other team. 'Whatever – we should give them a dose of their own medicine. They're a bunch of *dirty, fouling* –'

'MacB!' Mr Powell glared. His nostrils flared. 'Feelings are running high – I understand – but as captain, I expect you to set an example.' He took a long deep breath. 'We are *not* going to sink to their level. We are not going to play dirty. And we are not going to use foul or abusive language. Do I make myself clear?'

'Yes, sir.' Mac bowed his head. 'Sorry, sir.'

'We're all feeling angry, I'm sure,' said Mr Powell, 'but we mustn't let our emotions frustrate our objective. We are here to play quality football.'

Mr Powell turned slowly, eyeing each member of the team. 'The way forward, the way for us to get the upper hand, is through channelling that anger.' He balled his fist. 'Don't get mad, get even.'

'That's right!' Mac jumped to his feet. 'Come on, lads – let's show 'em.'

Shaking life back into stiffening limbs, the team made their way to their positions for the start of the second half.

Mac jogged up alongside Banksie. 'Terrific goals!' He draped his arm around Banksie's shoulders. 'Beauties. Both of them.'

Banksie stared, a little stunned. This was not what he'd come to expect. 'Thanks!' He smiled at his partner. 'Team work.'

'Yeah.' Mac smiled back. 'Let's make a few more!'

But things weren't quite that easy.

Within seconds of the kick, Banksie's ankles were chopped from beneath him, by a player he never even saw. Lying on the floor, his right ankle screaming, he heard both Mac and Mr Powell protesting in vain to the referee. But no whistle was blown.

As the game moved away towards St Dunstan's goal, Banksie staggered to his feet and tested his ankle.

'Is it all right?' Mr Powell beckoned from the touchline. 'I don't want to take you off, but it's no good playing on it, if it's sprained or twisted.'

Banksie winced and hobbled. 'I think it's just bruised, it's just where his boot whacked me.' He put more pressure on it. Cautiously he half skipped, half jogged to the centre line, then tried a short burst of speed. The ankle held up. He shot Mr Powell a thumbs up and moved into a forward position for the goal kick.

Gregg's kick came soaring high over the field. Mac had dropped back to help with the defence, now he powered up the field in front of the midfielders. Banksie was way out in front.

'Go on, Banksie!' yelled Mac. 'Run with it – take it all the way!'

Bringing the ball under control, Banksie began to accelerate. Slightly ahead of him, two defenders shadowed his every twist and swerve. They were the only players between him and the keeper, they seemed determined he shouldn't get past.

They were big for defenders and incredibly solid, given their speed. In the first half they had made sure he discovered that the hard way. Previous clashes had been bruising.

'Don't get cocky now, blondie.' The bigger of the two dropped a shoulder and barged him, hard. 'We don't like cocky,' he grunted.

Banksie shoved back.

Scarface, to his left, barged harder. 'You're for it!'

Slamming on the brakes, Banksie cut back and ran wide. The rest of the field were closing the gap. The wrong-footed defenders snarled and cursed. Now was the moment.

He charged for the goal, a heat-seeking missile locked on target. All he had to do was stay ahead and shoot. He had the edge – he was wide, but there was nothing between him and the keeper

'You're ours, blondie.'

'This time we're having you.'

Above the sound of his own gasping breath, his own thumping blood and pounding feet, he could hear them, centimetres behind.

'You've pushed us too far!'

'You're *dead*!'

He was close enough to tap it, but travelling too fast . . .

'Bye-bye, blondie.'

'It's been fun . . .'

'*Aaaaaaagh!*' Pain ripped through his legs.

The ground leapt up and smashed him in the face.

12

HOSPITAL

'We'd like to keep him under observation for a few days,' said Dr Wilson, a cheery-faced, greying man. 'Just a precaution. Everything looks fine, but where young people have suffered this degree of concussion, we like to monitor.'

Banksie glanced at his parents. They smiled.

'Now . . .' Dr Wilson flicked a switch.

It was only possible for Banksie to turn his head slowly. The drugs had muffled most of the pain, but his neck felt stiff, the muscles tight.

'These are the X-rays we took of your son's forearm.' Dr Wilson pointed to the ghostly shapes – two arm bones joining the wrist. 'You can see the fracture here. It's small and it's undisplaced. We're talking about a few weeks in the cast, maximum.'

'What about this?' Banksie tapped the plaster cast around his leg.

Dr Wilson smiled. 'That's just to immobilize your leg for a while, allow the inflammation around the joint to subside so your patella can make a proper recovery. We'll take it off when we remove the arm cast. Nothing to worry about in a healthy young boy.'

'Will I get to play football again?'

Dr Wilson chuckled. The grey wrinkles beneath his eyes pouched into dark bags. 'You shouldn't have any problems on that score! Once the casts are off, we'll have you up and running in no time.'

Banksie smiled at his mother.

His father winked.

The nurse parked the wheelchair at the foot of the bed.

After a moment, Dunk glanced up from the magazine he was reading. His mouth dropped and his eyes widened as if he was seeing a ghost. 'You!' he croaked. 'I don't believe it!'

Banksie grinned. 'How you doing?'

Dunk stared. 'This is some kind of a prank, right?'

Very gingerly, Banksie shook his head.

'Your eye . . .' Dunk frowned and pointed. 'Your arm . . . your leg . . . those bandages . . .

plaster casts . . . *the wheelchair*! It's all for real?'

''Fraid so,' said Banksie.

'I can't believe it,' said Dunk. 'You look . . . *terrible*.'

'Whereas you,' said Banksie, 'are a picture of health!'

Suddenly, the two of them were laughing. As their laughter grew louder and louder, other patients turned to stare. After a few moments, Dunk coughed, clutched his chest and panted for breath. 'Oh don't!' he gasped. 'We've got to stop.'

'You're telling me!' Banksie patted his bandaged head. 'It *hurts*!'

'This is really bad though,' gasped Dunk. 'What have you done?'

'I'm not as crippled as I look.' Banksie sighed. 'Not even in the same league as you.'

'Pah!' Dunk grinned and raised his chin in mock pride. 'Who is? But what happened?'

'Birnam Wood,' said Banksie.

'Birnam!'

Banksie nodded.

Dunk shook his head, grimly. 'Chances are, then, you were fouled.'

'How did you guess,' said Banksie. 'So many times, I lost count. The ref was blind.' He sliced the air with both hands. 'I got chopped from behind, two defenders at the same time. I hit the ground face first.'

'Ouch!'

'Synchronized shin-hacking.'

'An ancient-but-deadly skill,' said Dunk, 'honed to a fine art at that centre of excellence. I remember playing Birnam last year. They're the scum of the earth.'

Banksie nodded and smiled. 'In a league of their own.'

'They should be,' said Dunk. 'No one should have to play them.'

'The match was abandoned,' said Banksie. 'Everyone was really worried, apparently, Powelly especially. The fall knocked me out cold.'

'Nasty!'

'The headache came later,' said Banksie. 'When I came to, it was my leg and arm that really hurt. They were screaming agony, I thought they must both be broken.'

Dunk pulled a face as if sucking a lemon.

'Actually, it's not all that bad,' said Banksie. 'The shins are bruised and I've dislocated the knee cap, so I'm not going to be running around for a while.' He tapped the cast on his arm. 'Somewhere under this lot, there's a hairline fracture.'

'And the brain?' said Dunk.

'Bounced,' said Banksie, 'but not broken, apparently. They're keeping me in for observation and more tests. The doctor said I could be out of action for a few weeks.'

'A *few weeks*!' Dunk snorted. '*Hoh!* Come on, ref! Give me a break! I'm going to be stuck here, with my legs in the air, till well after blinking Christmas!'

'Yeah, I'm a lucky boy,' chuckled Banksie. 'I don't know if it'll be any consolation, but for the next few days I'm going to be keeping you company.' He patted the empty bed next to Dunk's.

Dunk beamed. 'Excellent.'

Banksie sighed. He rubbed his leg above the cast. 'It's already starting to itch.'

'Tell me about it!' Dunk let out a long groan. 'The itching drives you *mental*.'

'Look at your lovely cards and flowers,' said Nina.

Banksie groaned.

'Yeah,' said Shanice, 'and all this fruit! Poor boy's going to have a serious bowel condition if he eats this lot.' Taking a bunch of grapes from one of the bowls of fruit, she broke off small branches and handed them to her girlfriends. 'If he has to eat them all before he's allowed to leave, he could be here as long as poor Dunk.'

'Actually,' said Dunk, chuckling in his bed, 'I think finishing your fruit *is* one of the hospital rules.'

'You wish!' Banksie threw him a grape. 'You're just jealous because nobody brings you any.'

'Fruit starts to lose its appeal after a while,' said Dunk. 'I was never that keen in the first place. I think people began to catch on when it all started to rot.' He tapped the arm in a sling. 'Fruit's kind of tricky when only one arm's operational.'

'Perhaps you'd like some assistance?' said Nina. Sitting on the edge of Dunk's bed, she dangled a large bunch of grapes, tantalizingly, above his mouth. 'Would you like me to feed you?' she purred.

Dunk blushed. 'No one ever offered before.' He took a bite. '*Mmmm.*'

'Nina likes to do her bit to encourage healthy eating,' said Shanice. 'So, what do visitors bring long-stay patients that have grown bored of fruit?'

'Magazines,' spluttered Dunk, through a mouthful of grapes.

'*Magazines!*' exclaimed the three girls.

'Tons of them.' Dunk rapped his bedside cabinet.

'Hang on, sisters!' said Shanice. 'Don't get excited. We're talking *boys*, remember.' She opened the cabinet. Magazines and paperbacks spilled out on to the floor. 'Blimey, there's *loads*!'

'Yeah . . .' Dunk shrugged. 'Well . . . I have had the occasional moment with nothing to do.'

'Eat!' ordered Nina, pushing his jaw open and dangling in the grapes. 'You have to get your strength back.'

'Look at this lot!' said Shanice, down on her hands and knees. 'Football magazine . . . football magazine . . . cars . . . football . . . mountain bikes. See! What did I tell you?'

Eve joined her on the floor.

'*Angling Today* . . .?' said Shanice.

'No thanks!' said Eve. 'Oh, hang on! This looks interesting – *Martial Artist Monthly*.'

'Uh-oh,' said Shanice, 'the karate kid's happy. Don't you have any proper magazines – you know, like ones with fashion spreads and horoscopes and articles about celebrities?'

'And relationships,' added Nina, 'and hair and make-up?'

'Light, gossipy kind of stuff?' said Shanice.

'Ah!' said Banksie, spotting Mac at the end of the bed.

'Found one?' said Shanice.

'No.' Banksie pointed. 'Visitor.'

'Hello!' said Shanice, excitedly.

'Hi.' Mac's face was pale and drawn. He looked tired.

'Not you, stupid!' Shanice rolled her eyes. 'I just found a copy of *Hello!* magazine.'

Mac shrugged wearily. 'Well, hello anyway . . . everybody.'

'Good to see you,' said Banksie. 'I wondered when you were going to show up.'

'Yeah, sorry . . .' Mac shrugged again. 'I've not been feeling all that . . . I think I had the flu or something.'

'Perhaps you should book in here for a week,' said Dunk. 'At this rate we'll be taking over the ward!'

Mac nodded.

'I see you didn't come empty-handed,' said Shanice.

Nina and Eve tittered.

Mac glanced stupidly at his hands, dangling at his sides. 'My mum's just buying some flowers,' he said. 'We're not stopping.'

'It's all right,' said Banksie, 'I understand. Hospitals don't agree with you, do they, mate?'

Mac shook his head.

'But I'm grateful you came,' said Banksie. 'Don't let these three wind you up. You know what they're like.'

'What's your star sign?' said Shanice.

'What?' Mac looked puzzled.

'Your star sign – when you were born?' Shanice shook her head. 'Poor mite just isn't with it today, is he?'

'He's a Gemini, aren't you, darling?' Mrs MacBride and a large bouquet of flowers materialized behind her son. 'You'll have to forgive him, he's not been sleeping well. Actually, neither of us have. There are foxes in the neighbourhood and they've been keeping us poor souls awake with that awful, haunting, crying that they do.'

Mrs MacBride's face, as impeccably made-up as ever, showed little of the tiredness so evident in her son's.

'Gemini . . .' muttered Shanice, scanning the page, 'where are those twins?'

Squeezing past her, Mrs MacBride kissed Banksie on the cheek and handed him the bouquet.

'Thank you,' said Banksie. 'Lovely flowers. You're very kind.'

'Don't be silly,' said Mrs MacBride. She pointed to all the cards. 'It's good to see you've so many well-wishers. Plenty of visitors too?'

Banksie nodded. 'And having Dunk next door prevents me getting bored.'

'I suppose,' said Mrs MacBride, 'in a funny sort of way, the pair of you are quite lucky.' She chuckled. 'You're being well looked after, I hope?'

Banksie glanced across at Dunk. 'We'd both probably rather be outside kicking a ball, but . . .'

'The nurses are nice,' said Dunk. He blushed. 'Kind, I mean.'

'Good.' Mrs MacBride glanced at her watch. 'I'm sorry it's had to be such a brief visit.'

'Hang on,' said Shanice, waving the magazine, '. . . horoscope.'

'Oh yes, dear.' Mrs MacBride nudged her son. 'You'd like to hear your stars.'

'"Gemini",' read Shanice, '"With Saturn's conjunction to Mars at the start of the month, there are serious storm clouds brewing."' She threw Mac a nod. '"Batten down the hatches and take cover! Apart from a few days in the middle of the month, there will be little escape from the pressure. You already have your hands full, juggling work and home life, so avoiding that big clash is going to be difficult. Plenty of rest might be the way. A dark day when thirteen comes into play."'

Mac frowned.

'Sounds a bit heavy,' said Dunk.

'Yeah!' Banksie laughed and pointed to the magazine's cover. 'Good job the month's half over.'

'How *was* the thirteenth?' said Shanice.

Mac shrugged. 'Don't remember.'

'Load of rubbish, those horoscopes, anyway,' said Banksie.

'Come along,' said Mrs MacBride. She gave her son a little nudge. 'Say goodbye to your friends.'

Mac nodded. 'Cheers.'

Mrs MacBride smiled and waved. 'We'll be back before too long. Take care.'

'Yeah, *right*!' muttered Shanice, as Mac and his mum disappeared into the corridor. She shook her head. 'Like they're really going to return before you leave.'

'They might,' said Banksie, smiling, 'if they get back early tomorrow!'

'They couldn't wait to be out of here,' said Eve.

'They never even asked you about your injuries,' said Shanice.

'Yeah . . .' chuckled Dunk, 'they probably think you're here till next year, with poor old me!'

'Lovely flowers though,' said Nina, *'for a funeral.'*

13

FERNLEIGH

Banksie missed Dunk's company badly. The hospital had released him, but since St Dunstan's was hopeless for wheelchair access and, since half-term was now only a week away, his parents had decided he should stay at home.

His computer and a selection of his games, books, magazines, CDs and tapes had all been moved down from his bedroom. The lounge was his temporary residence, the sofa – his new bed. With the toilet downstairs, he had everything he needed.

A few days after he arrived home, Gregg popped round clutching a large bag of school books and homework in his big hands. But Banksie knew that till he went back to school after half-term, he was basically free to doss and do as he chose – watching telly, playing computer games, reading football stories, listening to music.

None of these things was what he really wanted though. He longed to be out playing football with his mates. But that wasn't possible. He kept reminding himself what the doctor had said about patience being important for a speedy recovery. In the meantime, he did have something to look forward to – St Dunstan's were playing at home the coming Saturday. And Dad had promised a lift.

His heart was pounding as he waved to his dad and wheeled away from the car. It had been a while since he'd been out in public, the fluttery feeling in his stomach was a mixture of excitement and nerves.

He was late. Whistles, shouts, and the sound of leather punishing leather, already filled the air. Games were in progress on most of the pitches. Where were the lads? Pulling up in front of the pavilion, he scanned the pitches for a clue to their whereabouts.

There! The telltale copper curls! And wouldn't you just know it – the game was right over on the pitch in the furthest corner. Banksie set off at his slow pace, rolling across the turf, thankful, at least, the ground wasn't boggy.

'Yes, yes, yes! *Goal!*' Even from a distance, the voice of Mrs MacBride rang clear across the playing field. *'Excellent!* That's my boy! *Come on, MacB!'*

It was a strange feeling, to be on the outside again, on a playing field again; stranger still to be an outsider, watching, not participating.

The fresh clean strips were already mud-spattered. Fernleigh, in their dazzling all-orange, took a quick kick and pushed deep into St Dunstan's half on the counter-attack. With assistance from Oliver and Ridley, St Dunstan's backs were fighting hard to hold them off.

'Get that ball out!' bellowed Mac, from the centre line.

'Come on!' yelled Mr Powell from the touchline. 'Let's not waste a glorious start. Turn this ball around!'

A tall, dark-haired Fernleigh forward received the ball from the wing. McAllister charged in for the tackle. The Fernleigh forward stumbled, but hung on to the ball and, recovering his balance, pushed on towards St Dunstan's goal.

Gregg hunkered down, ready for the shot. Woddis, his shiny dome no higher than the attacker's shoulder, harried again and again from the side. Lurking in the background, Patel and Oliver waited for an opportunity to tackle. Suddenly, Ridley swung in from the side, slid along the ground and, in a perfectly timed swipe, hacked the ball away to Patel.

'*Yes!*' yelled Mac.

'Nice play!' yelled Mr Powell. 'Now *keep* possession.'

'Go on!' yelled Mrs MacBride. 'Go *on*!'

Second touch, Patel had passed the ball, low but long, back across to the right. In a flash, Terry Eaton was transformed from wilting flower to sprinting cheetah – legs churning, body lurching, ball at his feet. In seconds, the field had been left standing.

Banksie cheered. He wanted to leap up and clap, but had to content himself with punching the air. Now that he'd finally reached the pitch, he could identify the new member of the team – the very compact Daniel Tovey. Normally a defensive or midfield player, Tovey was chasing Mac towards the Fernleigh goal. On the far side, keeping pace, Jamie Wallace swung in towards the centre.

A defender beat Mac to the cross, clearing with a desperate volley. But doubling back, Jamie Wallace followed the ball and, with a volley of his own, kept it from going into touch.

'What happened to *control*?' yelled Mr Powell.

Beating off the competition, Tovey reclaimed the wild ball for St Dunstan's. Fernleigh's midfield harried. Tovey dodged and turned, and turned again. He kept his head.

'Dan!' Mac signalled for the ball and tried to throw off his marker.

Tovey dummied back to Wallace on the wing, then, twisting sharply, lobbed the ball into the box. Mac found it with his knee, brought it down. He danced it – first one way, then the other – round one defender, then another. Then another.

The St Dunstan's supporters shouted and cheered.

Banksie held his breath.

Mac dummied to the right post.

The keeper dived.

Mac swerved sharply left and, hands clasped triumphantly above his head, *dribbled* the ball into the net.

The supporters *roared*.

And so the first half continued – with Fernleigh making repeated attempts to regain the initiative, but getting knocked back again and again by the increasingly confident home side. St Dunstan's *fourth* goal came from a penalty. With the deadly accuracy he was now famous for, Mac blasted it for his hat-trick. As Fernleigh's keeper picked the ball out of the net, Mac ran to be mobbed by his teammates.

Having by now wheeled his way along the touchline to where the largest cluster of parents stood alongside Mr Powell, Banksie joined in the yelling and hooting, for all he was worth.

Woddis, Ridley and Oliver cavorted and jumped around their captain. Mac turned and twisted playfully, swerved and ran, pursued by the others towards St Dunstan's half.

'MacB!' yelled Banksie. 'MacB!'

Turning, fist raised, to acknowledge the home supporters, Mac suddenly stumbled to a stop. He stood, mouth gaping, staring.

As Banksie grinned, he saw Mac's puzzled expression darken. Then, just as sharply as he'd stopped, Mac spat at the ground and jogged off.

Banksie felt numb. In spite of warm clothes and a blanket, he shivered. *What was wrong? What had happened? What was Mac so furious about?*

He tried to watch the game. Fernleigh were stealing it back. Mac's flare had evaporated. Whatever he attempted now, he fluffed. Again and again he mis-kicked the ball, fell over his own feet, shot wide of the goal, or got caught off-side.

The referee's decisions went against Mac. The passes stopped coming. All he seemed able to do was shout. Fernleigh tightened their hold till, finally, it was their turn to score.

But that was just the beginning. Straightaway, they scored again. And, on the half-time whistle, their tall, dark striker blasted number three between the posts. Three goals in under ten minutes. St Dunstan's confidence was on the floor in tatters.

Storming from the pitch, Mac barged past Mr Powell and through the small crowd of parents. Red-faced and shaking with rage, he halted in front of Banksie.

The green eyes narrowed to tiny slits, they looked meaner than Banksie could ever remember.

'All right!' yelled Mac, grabbing the wheelchair armrests. He thrust his face up close. *'What are you playing at?'*

'What?' Banksie clenched the wheel with his good hand. 'What do you mean?'

'You!' Mac's face contorted, he was *spitting* with rage. 'You shouldn't be here.'

'What?'

'You're supposed to be . . . I don't know.' Mac looked suddenly confused. 'You're staring at me the whole time like . . . like . . .' He jabbed a finger. *'What's your little game?'*

Banksie wiped his face. 'What are you going on about?'

Players and parents were staring.

Mac thrust an arm towards the pitch. 'What

am I supposed to do? Sit around and wait for you to get better? It's not my fault you're out of action.'

'I never said it was!' Banksie shook his head in disbelief. 'I just came along to support the team!'

Mac snorted and tapped the side of his head. 'I'm not stupid you know.'

'What?'

'You'd like to spoil my success.'

'What!'

'Oh yes!' Mac nodded, furiously. 'I know why you showed up.'

'What? What are you talking about!'

'That's enough!' Mrs MacBride appeared, panting. She had, apparently, hurried across the pitch from where she'd been standing. She wrapped her arms around Mac's chest. 'Ignore him,' she said, turning to the watching parents. She chuckled. 'He's just overheating.'

Banksie could see the tension in Mac's eyes. His knuckles were clenched as he tried to jerk himself free from his mother's grip.

But quick as a flash, Mrs MacBride caught his wrist. Still smiling, she tugged him closer. She bent to whisper in his ear.

Banksie watched her lips. *You're embarrassing me*, was it? *Be a man*?

She ruffled her son's hair and touched his

sweaty brow. *'Tsssh!'* she hissed. *'Hot!* First you get made team captain. And now, all of a sudden, solo striker too. The pressure's getting to you, isn't it?' She eased her grip. 'Come on – calm down. You should be with your teammates. Go and join them . . . get yourself a drink.'

Mac glared at Banksie one last time. *'You shouldn't be here,'* he hissed. 'Stop trying to ruin my game!'

'I'm sorry!' Mrs MacBride apologized again to the parents, looking flustered as she moved among them.

Banksie was shaking when Mr Powell came hurrying over. 'I don't know what's come over MacB,' he said. 'It must be the shock of seeing you in a wheelchair like that. He seems very distressed. I think a lot of people thought you'd be stuck in hospital quite a while. I only just heard you were out, myself.' He frowned. 'Are you all right?'

Banksie nodded. 'Just cold. I think I'll watch the second half from the pavilion.'

'D'you need someone to give you a push?' said Mr Powell.

'No, I'll manage,' said Banksie. Straightening the blanket over his knees, he forced a smile. 'I need the exercise.'

'Everyone's missed you,' said Mr Powell. He

winked. 'Good to see you up and about so soon.'

The change of fortunes in the second half was as dramatic as that of the first. Through binoculars borrowed from the groundsman, Banksie watched Mac's confidence gradually return. He witnessed a run of extraordinary success – passes arrived straight at Mac's feet, Mac's own passes travelled exactly where intended. And time and again, the referee seemed to give him the benefit of the doubt.

But through Banksie's eyes the world looked increasingly pinched and dreary. A heavy winter blanket of dismal grey had rolled its way across the sky. The change in St Dunstan's fortunes could do nothing to shift his gloom. Something was wrong. Something was seriously wrong. The ugly clash with Mac on the touchline had left him feeling worse than he could remember. There was a bitter taste in his mouth. His stomach churned. He was angry of course. No – not just angry, he was *furious*. But it was more than that.

He shivered. There had always been little things about Mac that had unsettled him, made him uncomfortable. But now, after Mac's outburst and his mother's reaction, he was left with a deep feeling of unease. The more he replayed the scene, the more he thought about events of the past few weeks – the more his mind kept returning to the fortune-teller's prophesy. In his heart of hearts, he didn't believe prediction was possible. But there was no denying his sense of doom.

Out on the pitch, a light drizzle was falling. But every shot from Mac's boot was on target. And, in spite of his courageous keeping, Fernleigh's goalie failed to keep a single one out. The final, incredible score was eight goals to three. Six of St Dunstan's had been scored by Mac.

The mud-covered team lifted Mac on to their shoulders. As they trotted in triumph towards the pavilion, Banksie sloped off to the gates to wait for his father.

14
HALF-TERM

'Look at that!' said Shanice.

The man in the white coat smiled and began to cut into the plaster with the small circular saw.

Banksie squirmed and glanced at his mum.

'He's going to cut off your leg,' said Shanice. 'Then he's going to cut off your arm!'

'*Shanice . . .*'

The man chuckled. 'Your daughter's got a lively imagination,' he said. He winked at Banksie. 'They're specially designed, these saws. It can't cut you – rest assured.'

'He's gone terribly pale though,' said Shanice. 'He looks like a ghost.'

'Shut up,' said Banksie.

'Both of you,' said Mum.

'Don't worry,' said the man. 'I'll be cutting through the tubigrip with scissors. We'll get you to come back at the end of half-term, so the physio can check everything's OK. OK?'

Banksie nodded.

'Forty-one ... forty-two ...' Banksie twisted and caught the ball with the back of his heel. He ducked. The ball came over. He hit it with his right thigh. 'Forty-three ...' With his left. 'Forty-four ...' Heads. 'Forty-five ...' And again. 'Forty-six ...' Down to the left instep, a controlled tap. 'Forty-seven ...' Across to the right. 'Forty-eight ...' He held it there. Flipped it. Span on his left toe. Caught the ball back on the right. 'Forty-*nine* ...'

'There doesn't appear to be much wrong with *you*!'

Banksie turned. 'Mr Powell!'

'Hi.' He held out his hands.

Banksie flipped him the ball.

'Excellent! I've just been to visit poor old Duncan. I thought I'd pop in to check how our other invalid was getting on. Your sister told me to come out and see for myself.'

'What d'you reckon?' Banksie raised his chin and lifted his arms, as if to say 'here I am'! Taking three short skipping steps, he sprang, cartwheeled and *flipped*.

'*Whoa!*' Mr Powell looked shocked. 'Last time I saw you, you were in a wheelchair, with your arm and leg in plaster – now you're doing arab-springs. Are you supposed to do that stuff?'

Banksie laughed and shrugged. 'I wasn't sure I still could!' He squatted on the grass, still giddy. 'I have to go back to the hospital tomorrow. With a bit of luck, they'll be giving me the all-clear.'

'That's excellent news. So you'll be back at school after half-term?'

Banksie nodded. 'It'll be hard after such a long break, but yep – Monday morning, with all the others.'

'It's a shame you can't play for us tomorrow,' said Mr Powell. 'I could do with some extra players. I've got a couple off sick, we're down to one sub.'

'I'd like to,' said Banksie.

'I don't think so.' Mr Powell frowned. 'It's Birnam Wood.'

'Of course!' said Banksie. 'The abandoned match. I'd give my right arm –'

Mr Powell raised an eyebrow. 'I'd rephrase that, if I were you.'

'Whoops!' said Banksie. 'I mean I'd *love* a chance to play.'

'The two louts responsible for your injury are on a suspension, but even if you had the doctor's permission, I'm not sure I'd feel happy putting you back in the side against Birnam.'

He shook his head. 'It's never wise to tempt fate.'

'You've seen how well I've recovered.' Banksie rubbed his knee. 'My appointment's early. What if the physio says I'm fit?'

Mr Powell laughed. 'We'll see. You're keen – that's for sure! The team'll be delighted to hear you're mended.'

'Actually,' said Banksie, 'I'd rather you didn't say anything till I've been for my check-up. I know it's sort of superstitious,' he grinned, 'but like you said – best not to tempt fate.'

Mr Powell nodded. 'Good luck with it then.'

'And good luck with the match,' said Banksie. 'Let's hope that this time there's a result!'

15

REPLAY

Shanice held open the door. She frowned. 'Why am I still doing this?'

Banksie grinned. 'Good habits die hard.'

'Believe me,' said Shanice, 'that was my last lapse. You should be holding doors open for me.' She jabbed him in the back.

'Ow!'

'Especially now,' said Shanice. 'You heard what the physio said: *full working order*.' She jabbed him again. '*Shirker!*'

'Get lost!' Banksie laughed. 'I have to admit, it was nice – you treating me as human for a change. But it's great being able to run around again.'

'You do realize,' said Shanice, 'your little legs keep breaking into a skip? I know you're chuffed about being given the green light and everything. But could you try and control yourself, please? At your age! People are *staring*.'

Banksie did a little jump and clicked his heels together. He grinned. 'I'll try.'

'Tell you what!' Jerking her brother towards an empty wheelchair, Shanice jumped into the seat. 'You can return the favour – I pushed you around enough.'

'Still do!' laughed Banksie.

'Less of the cheek, slave!' Shanice folded her arms and settled back. 'Come on, it's my turn for a bit of pampering. *Push!*'

'Which way then?' said Banksie.

Shanice pointed

'What! The main entrance?'

'Uh-huh.'

'There's a security guard . . .'

'Then don't act like a lemon.'

Stroking his moustache, the guard scrutinized their approach.

Banksie smiled and tried to look relaxed.

The guard yawned.

Then they were through the doors and away. 'Freedom!' yelled Shanice as they careened down the ramp. They laughed their way across the car park to the main gates.

'Fresh air!' gasped Banksie.

'*Fresh* is right,' said Shanice. 'More of a cold breeze actually.' She nodded towards the sky. Slate-coloured clouds were massing, layer upon layer, into a threatening configuration.

'We should get a move on.'

'It's a battleship!' said Banksie. 'No – a giant aircraft carrier, towering above the hospital!'

'Whatever.' Shanice wiped her forehead. 'Can we scoot, please. I just felt a spot of rain.'

The cloud formation followed, mushrooming and darkening to a sludgy, yellow-grey. Fifteen minutes after leaving the hospital, the wheelchair, with Banksie in the passenger seat and Shanice once again at the helm, bowled down the pavilion driveway.

'You're breaking the speed limit!' gasped Banksie, clutching the armrests.

'Rubbish!' said Shanice. 'I thought you were in a hurry?'

'I am, but I'd like to arrive in one piece! *Look out!*' As Banksie shut his eyes, the wheelchair hit the hump, full tilt, and left the ground.

'Handles like a dream!' panted Shanice. '*Hang on*, there's another coming up!'

Three humps later, they reached the pavilion. Banksie was gibbering.

'I don't know what you're complaining about,' said Shanice. 'I had to put up with broken paving stones, potholes, kerbs – the lot.'

'Remind me,' groaned Banksie, opening his eyes, 'never to accept a lift from you, if ever you learn to drive.'

On the playing field in front of them, only one pitch was in use.

Banksie wheeled the chair on to the grass. 'Come on,' he said, 'that must be us.'

'How d'you work that out, Einstein?'

Banksie ignored Shanice's sarcasm. 'There's no fixtures over half-term. This match is a replay.'

'Looks like quite a crowd,' said Shanice. 'Well, more than the handful you usually get.'

'It's a grudge match,' said Banksie. 'After what happened last time, everyone at St Dunstan's wants to see Birnam get slaughtered.'

'You lot? Slaughter Birnam?' Shanice shook her head. 'In your dreams!'

'We can do it,' said Banksie. 'There's loads of talent in the side. Mac's an exceptional player . . . and a captain to be reckoned with.'

'You sound really convinced.'

Banksie paused. His arms ached already from pushing the wheels on soft ground. He shrugged. 'He has been acting a bit weird recently.'

'Recently?' Shanice laughed. 'That boy's *always* been weird!'

They had reached the nearest corner of the pitch. In front of the goal, big Jake Gregg watched events down the other end. Parents and boys from St Dunstan's were scattered along the touchline, shouting and cheering; a bigger cluster had gathered at the midpoint. Birnam Wood's supporters faced them on the opposite side.

Most people appeared to be very well wrapped: in coats and scarves, puffa jackets and caps, waterproofs and woollen hats. Here and there, occasional anxious faces glanced heavenward; the cold breeze appeared to have died, but the thunderous clouds were darkening by the minute. Umbrellas began to sprout.

Banksie squinted. Two familiar figures were standing at the back, among the mums and dads. Cosgrove and his colleague, the detectives from school.

'Oi, dreamboy!' Shanice tapped his shoulder. 'What you gawping at? Are we going to find your coach or what? All that urgency to get here.'

'Just a minute,' said Banksie. The fluttery feeling was back in his stomach. 'I need to check out the game.'

A quick scan of the players confirmed what Mr Powell had told him – there was no sign of the two thugs whose tackles had left him injured.

St Dunstan's were on the attack. Apart from

a couple of players hovering in the centre, Birnam were all back, defending. For them to be this cautious, St Dunstan's had to have been playing well.

'Come on, St Dunstan's!' yelled the home supporters. 'Time for another!'

Banksie turned to the man next to him. 'Have there been goals already?'

'Certainly have, son – it's one–all.' The man nodded towards Birnam's crowded penalty area. 'The red-headed youth scored ours.'

Outmanoeuvring two Birnam players on the touchline, Jamie Wallace lofted the ball into the box.

'MacB! MacB! MacB!' St Dunstan's supporters chanted, in one loud voice.

Five players leapt to meet the cross, but it was Mac who reached it. His header powered past helpless defenders to ricochet off the post. It flew straight back to him. He met it with a furious rocket volley.

'YEEEES!' Banksie leapt into the air.

The home crowd went potty.

'Not bad!' said Shanice.

'Mac's a chuffing genius!' said Banksie. 'Come on, let's go and find Mr Powell.'

The two teams jogged back to their positions ready for the kick.

Trotting along the touchline in front of the

supporters, Mr Powell yelled encouragement to the team. 'We're doing great! Don't get complacent now – we've got to keep up the pressure.'

Supporters stepped aside as Banksie manoeuvred his way through the crowd.

'Oh!' Mrs MacBride froze. 'What a lovely surprise. Banksie! *And* your lovely sister.' She smiled. 'Both of you've come to watch – he'll be delighted.'

Banksie nodded. 'Sounds like a great game.'

'Come through to the front,' said Mrs MacBride. 'We must get you a good viewpoint.'

'Come on!' bellowed Mr Powell. 'They're tough, and now they're two–one down they're getting *frustrated*. Watch out for the rough stuff. We all know what they're capable of.'

As Banksie parked up beside him, a darkened portion of the sky erupted in dazzling flashes.

The crowd gasped and grunted.

'Hey!' yelled Jamie Wallace, ignoring the lightning. 'Look who's here!'

'*Banksie!*' Cheers rose up from the team.

As Banksie waved, an enormous, earth-shaking sound rolled out of the clouds.

People flinched and covered their ears.

In the centre of the pitch, Mac nodded stiffly and turned away.

The whistle blew. Birnam Wood took their kick, passing the ball out to the far side. Mac and Terry Eaton closed in. The winger passed back. Mac chased.

'Come on, St Dunstan's!'

Mac harried one midfielder after another as they passed the ball across the pitch.

Banksie felt a hand on his shoulder.

'You're in a wheelchair,' said Mr Powell. His eyes remained glued to the pitch.

'Oh . . .' Banksie shrugged. 'It's . . . er . . . borrowed.'

Mr Powell raised an eyebrow.

'I thought one last appearance in a wheelchair might inspire the lads,' said Banksie, 'sort of remind them of what's at stake.'

Mr Powell smiled. 'Our sub's on already.' He nodded towards the pitch. 'Had to take Tovey off after six minutes. Twisted ankle. I've moved Woddis up to fill the gap and put Marshall in at left-back.'

'I'm ready to play,' said Banksie, 'if you need me.' He squinted towards the pitch. As the storm clouds rolled overhead, light was growing steadily dimmer – it was becoming increasingly hard to follow the action.

The pace of battle had quickened: Birnam Wood had broken through the centre. With ever-increasing confidence their forwards passed and ran, passed and ran. Now St Dunstan's were wavering. As one after another, Oliver, Woddis, Ridley and McAllister attempted and failed to intercept, the rest of the team fell back.

From his goal area, Gregg directed defenders with yells and grunts.

'Come on,' bellowed Mac, chasing Birnam's advance. '*Tackle* them! Get stuck in!'

'*Come on, St Dunstan's!*' Banksie chanted with the crowd.

'The bigger they are, the harder they fall!' yelled Mrs MacBride. 'Take them down! *Cripple* them!'

Banksie caught his coach's glance.

Mr Powell shrugged. 'The ref's already had words with her. I've asked her to tone it down.'

'Go on, MacB!' bayed Mrs MacBride. 'Go on, my son!'

'MacB!' the crowd echoed, 'Mac*B*!'

Into the penalty area, the three Birnam's ploughed forward. St Dunstan's midfield were in disarray.

Fuelled by the crowd's fervour, charging like a madman, Mac had all but caught up. '*Tackle*, for crying out loud!' he roared. '*Tackle!*'

Jamie Wallace seemed to accelerate from out of nowhere.

'Don't leave it to each other!' yelled Mac. 'TACKLE!'

Spurred by his captain's excitement, Jamie Wallace leapt and stretched a foot to the ball.

From the opposite side, Mac hurled himself.

As lightning ripped through the charcoal sky, the Birnam player swerved.

Mac and Jamie collided in a brief, high-speed embrace; their bodies span and flew apart.

The crowd gasped. The whistle blew. Mr Powell raced on to the pitch.

Banksie caught a glimpse of Mrs MacBride, hands to face, pale. Her brow furrowed. Suddenly, she cupped her hands round her mouth. 'Come on, MacB!' she yelled. 'Don't let a little knock put you down.'

This time the thunder crack was loud. *Really* loud. Heads ducked, there were fearful squeals, and a small baby began to cry. The storm was close.

Waving frantically, the ref tried to push back players who had gathered round their colleagues on the ground. With one arm draped round Mr Powell, and one round Terry Eaton, Jamie Wallace limped towards the touchline.

'Banks,' yelled Mr Powell, 'the bag's on the floor – hurry up and get your kit on.' Leaving

Wallace to limp in with Eaton, he turned and ran back.

Jumping up from the wheelchair, Banksie flung off his clothes and began dragging on kit. Supporters nudged one another and stared open-mouthed. He felt electric. 'I owe you,' he sniggered, as Shanice helped tie his laces.

'You're not wrong! You owe me *big time*!' She slapped the finished boot and passed him a shirt. 'It's the only one left – thirteen!'

Banksie shrugged. 'Unlucky for some.'

Mac was now standing among the huddled players. Mr Powell was examining his bowed head.

As Banksie hurried across the pitch, pulling on the shirt, the first fat drops of rain splattered his skin like overripe grapes.

Looking up, Mac froze.

Players turned.

Banksie smiled and nodded. 'I'm fit to play!'

Mac shook his head. *'No!'* he spat. The eyes flashed fury. 'You *can't* be!' He barged his way through the gathered players.

Banksie halted, his legs had turned to lead.

'MacB . . .' Mr Powell placed a hand against Mac's shoulder.

Mac paused, considering Mr Powell's hand. His expression appeared to soften. Then with a sudden twist, he snapped his shoulder away. *'I am captain!'* he yelled, lurching towards Banksie. *'You* can't be!'

Banksie stared, baffled. *What was Mac on about?*

Mac strode closer. 'I am still captain!' He jabbed a finger. 'I'm captain, *hear me*?'

Banksie wanted to nod, but he was paralysed.

'You will never replace me!' Mac spat his words. 'Never! I'm a better player and captain than you could ever be.'

Banksie felt himself sway. His mouth had dried. The fortune teller had said something about *one captains first, the other thereafter . . .* Was *that* what he was raving about? The prophesy?

'MacB . . .' Mrs MacBride called from the crowd. *'MacB!'*

Mac gobbed at the ground . . . thrust his face close.

Banksie blinked, twitched.

'You were *crippled,'* shouted Mac, shoving him hard.

Banksie staggered back.

Mac grabbed his shirt. 'It was *arranged,'* he hissed, jabbing a finger towards the Birnam supporters.

'What?' croaked Banksie. Arranged? He couldn't believe what he was hearing. *Had Mac flipped?*

'MacB!' Mrs MacBride ran towards her son. 'What's wrong with you?'

'It's all right . . . it's *all right*!' Mac shooed her away.

'MacB, *listen* to me!' she snapped. 'Will you listen to me, please? Don't go making a fool of yourself . . . don't go making fools of us in front of all these people.'

'Making fools?' Mac chuckled. 'It's all right, Mum . . . I know what I'm doing.' His face twitched. 'Don't worry! I'm in control. I'm *captain*, remember.'

'Listen to your mother.' Mrs MacBride held out her hands. 'Come on, MacB . . . you've done enough talking. That's enough!' She lunged.

Mac jerked his arm away.

'You're rambling,' she said, 'you've had a knock . . .' Her hands clutched and clutched again. 'You need to rest.'

'Mum!' Mac yanked free. *'Don't!'* He grabbed Banksie by the elbow, twisted him. 'There! look!' Again he jabbed a finger towards the Birnam supporters. 'Look . . . at the end there . . . see?'

The light had grown so dim, Banksie had to crane his neck and peer.

'You're being stupid!' said Mrs MacBride. 'Poor Banksie was knocked unconscious, he's not going to remember.'

Banksie squinted. At the far end of the supporters, two figures were doing their best to look small and inconspicuous. There was a sudden flash. A streak of pure white arced down the sky. In the glow, he recognized the two Birnam tacklers who had injured him. Scarface and the other one. They stared at their feet.

'See them?' urged Mac.

A deafening thunderclap accompanied Banksie's nod.

'What are you doing?' Mrs MacBride grabbed her son's arm.

'Guess!' Mac broke free and dodged sideways. Again he pointed towards the two Birnam boys. 'Go on, Banksie . . . *guess*.'

Banksie stared. Guess? *What was he supposed to guess?*

The sky flashed again.

'MacBride!' The larger of the two boys made a gesture – slicing his throat with a finger. 'Keep your mouth *shut*, MacBride.'

'You *know* them?' gasped Banksie. The question was punctuated by an ear-splitting *crack*.

Mac chuckled. 'Better than that!'

'MacB!' Mrs MacBride lunged and caught her son's shirt. 'You've gone *far enough*!'

Mac leered. 'Come on, Banksie . . .' He made

a gesture with his hand, rubbing his fingers against his thumb. 'Guess!'

'Money?' said Banksie. 'What are you saying? You *paid* them?'

'Wha-hey! Very good!' Mac jerked and flapped, struggling to break free of his mother. There was a ripping sound. Mrs MacBride kept her hold. 'Stop this!' she shrieked. 'Stop it, you idiot! Do you want to ruin everything?'

'Mother!' Mac giggled. 'You're tearing my kit!'

Rain was pitter-pattering, falling faster.

'You *paid* those two thugs?' said Banksie. 'To deliberately . . . *injure* me?' Not Mac. Not his mate. Not the boy he'd trained with all summer long. Banksie shook his head. 'I don't believe you.'

Mac shrugged. Suddenly, he ducked and broke lose from his mother. 'Guess!' He laughed. 'Guess where the money came from!'

'Don't listen to him!' shrieked Mrs MacBride. 'He's sick! Don't listen to him!'

'Mummy darling!' Mac grinned. 'You look after me, don't you?'

Mrs MacBride scowled furiously.

'Where else would I get the money?' yelled Mac. He waved towards the two Birnam thugs. One stepped forwards shaking a fist. 'You ask them,' gasped Mac. 'We paid *good* money!'

Lightning snaked down the sky. The fist-shaker cowered. A thunderclap exploded directly overhead. And, suddenly, rain began to pour. People screamed and ran for cover.

Mrs MacBride stumbled towards her son. 'Idiot!' she shrieked. 'Idiot! Idiot! Idiot!'

Mac laughed, water streaming down his face. 'It's OK, Mother!'

'Shut *up*!' shrieked Mrs MacBride. 'Everything I've done, I've done for you!'

'Motherly love!' laughed Mac. 'All for me!'

The rain fell more heavily still, and faster.

'Without me,' yelled Mrs MacBride, 'none of your success, none of your glory would have been possible. None of it!'

'So true.' Mac grinned.

'You are *stupid*!' Rivulets of mascara ran, like black tears, down Mrs MacBride's cheeks; her lank, bedraggled hair clung to her face. 'But worse,' she shrieked, struggling to make herself heard over the downpour's roar, 'you're *gutless*. I didn't just give you money, I gave you *fire . . . I gave you the strength to do the things you had to.*'

Banksie watched Mac's face twitch.

Mrs MacBride pushed her son. 'So when I say shut up, you DO IT.'

Mac stared. He frowned. His shoulders slumped.

Mrs MacBride was shaking.

Suddenly, Mac burst out laughing. 'You don't understand!'

'*Shut up!*' Mrs MacBride clutched her ears and shook her head.

'Mother . . . you're missing the point!' Mac threw his arms wide. 'Nothing can stop me now! The dark day has passed. I'm still captain!'

'The dark and bloody day,' groaned Mrs MacBride, through clenched teeth. 'Your *stupid* prophesy!'

Mac turned. 'Banksie . . .' He shook his head. 'Sorry, mate . . . you had to be removed.' The green eyes flashed as lightning split the sky.

'Idiot!' squealed Mrs MacBride.

Banksie felt his knees shake; his heart pounded louder than the thunder. He opened his mouth, but rain water flooded in. No words.

'Not just you,' Mac laughed, 'but dear old Dunk of course too.'

Mrs MacBride screamed and dropped to her knees. She began to sob.

Emerging from the rain, two figures staggered forward, grabbed Mrs MacBride's arms and tried to help her up.

Mac plunged towards Banksie, feet splashing. 'You see!' he shrieked. 'No one can touch me now. *The dark day when thirteen comes into play* was more than two weeks ago. The thirteenth!'

'You're talking about the horoscope?' said Banksie.

Mac nodded. 'And the prophesy. It's all one and the same – the dark day when my captaincy might have been snatched.' He sneered. 'But you missed your chance. The day slipped by, completely unnoticed.' He thrust his arms heavenwards, threw back his head and laughed. 'Captain now! Captain for *ever*!'

'You're insane!' yelled Banksie. But the rain was too heavy and Mac too busy laughing to hear. It was like being under water. He turned, trying to wipe water from his eyes, peering through the murk. Mrs MacBride had been helped to her feet and, escorted by one of her helpers, was heading towards the pavilion along with his sister and the last of the hurrying, rain-soaked supporters. He glimpsed the face of the man escorting her. It was the thinner of the two detectives.

Then it happened. Right in front of him, a dazzling fork of light ripped down from the sky. It was as if Nature had been unzipped, unleashing some immeasurable force. The goalposts began spitting showers of brilliant sparks. The air around him crackled. His skin prickled. His nostrils filled with a harsh, burning smell. The goalposts flashed several times, like faltering fluorescent tubes, then finally, ear-shatteringly, *exploded*.

For a moment he thought he'd died. But he could hear Mac's voice, raging in the rain. He opened his eyes and lifted himself from the mud.

'No!' Mac was screaming. *'It can't be!'* Looking and sounding like some frantic injured bird, he hopped up and down, clutching his face with one hand, pointing with the other.

Pointing, Banksie realized, at him. He scrambled to his feet.

'Thirteen!' shrieked Mac. *'Thirteen!'* Suddenly, he charged.

Banksie threw himself sideways, but not fast enough. Mac's arm caught him round the throat and swung him off balance. He staggered and grabbed Mac's arm.

'It's *you*!' screamed Mac. *'You're* number thirteen – the shirt! *You* came into play. In spite of everything, *it's YOU*!'

As Banksie raised an arm to fend off the blows, Mac lunged, grabbed hold of his collar and with one violent yank, shrieked and flung himself at the ground. The shirt ripped.

Mac didn't get up.

Banksie watched his friend shake. He was shaking too. His fists and teeth were clenched. He hugged himself.

There was someone standing beside him in the rain. He turned.

Cosgrove.

The big detective nodded. 'I'll take care of everything now,' he said. Slowly he crouched, to kneel where Mac lay sobbing in the mud. Wiping rain from his face and glasses, he nodded up at Banksie. 'You OK, son?'

Banksie was still shaking; shaking uncontrollably. He managed a shrug. 'I think so.'

'Bit shocked, I should imagine.' Cosgrove smiled. 'Things aren't usually this lively when you get on the pitch then?'

Banksie shook his head.

'Don't worry,' said Cosgrove, 'we witnessed it all.' Lifting Mac's arm, he neatly snapped handcuffs around the wrist. 'Come on,' he grunted. 'On your feet, son. The fun and games are over.'

In the crushing rain, as lightning slashed the darkness, Cosgrove struggled to heft his prisoner from the ground. Banksie caught a final glimpse of Mac, half-lurching, half-crawling, dragged along in the big man's wake. That was it then? All that talent, that blazing energy and determination, all that burning ambition, reduced to something pitiful, stumbling through the mud?

Thunder cracked, rumbled and rolled into the distance.

That was it.

A white shape in the mud caught Banksie's eye. He jogged over. It was the ball. He lifted it with his toe, whacked it high, and broke into a blind run.

The rain pelting his face seemed to slacken as he sped. The tiniest chink of clear sky opened on the horizon. The storm, at last, was moving on.